THE BEST SUBSTITUTE EVER

AS TOLD BY A FIFTH GRADER

by

DANIEL GALT

Let your tidal wave of imagination
free; nothing can stop it!

Daniel Galt

TELEMACHUS PRESS

The publisher does not have any control over and does not assume any responsibility for author or third-party websites or their content.

Cover designed by Telemachus Press, LLC

Cover art by Daniel Galt

Published by Telemachus Press, LLC
http://www.telemachuspress.com

Visit the author's Facebook page:
www.facebook.com/DanielGaltBooksLLC/

ISBN: 978-1-942899-53-2 (eBook)
ISBN: 978-1-942899-54-9 (Paperback)

Version 2015.11.09

10 9 8 7 6 5 4 3 2 1

ACKNOWLEDGEMENT

I want to thank Mom for her help and encouragement, and my aunts, Duff, Pam, and Julie, for their financial support in getting my first book published. Also, I dedicate this book to all the students I have taught as both a special education and substitute teacher.

TABLE OF CONTENTS

THE BEST SUBSTITUTE EVER

AS TOLD BY A FIFTH GRADER

INTRODUCTION

Follow student Gregory Gaines as he tells what happened when he was a fifth grader at Workaholic Elementary School. Like it or not, substitutes are a part of school, and I bet you've had one that you really liked. This story is about a special substitute, and his name is Mr. Prosper. By the time you finish reading this book, I know you'll want him at your school, too!

Chapter 1
Introduction: Mr. Prosper

GOOD MORNING, AFTERNOON, or evening, whenever you happen to be reading this tale about Mr. Prosper, the best substitute teacher ever, as told to you by a fifth grade student. It's currently afternoon for me, and I have decided to tell this non-fiction tale because I truly believe it should be heard.

By the way, my name is Gregory Gaines. I was the head student photographer and video editor at our school this year. I took over the reins from Ashton Andrews, last year's lead photographer and video editor. I have always been told I knew more about video editing than Mrs. Quest, my supervisor and school librarian. In addition to those exciting jobs, I was also the chief editor of photography for the yearbook. Because I was so quiet, yeah *that* kind of guy, nobody at school knew I was in the room unless I said something. I usually only spoke up when I got in *the zone*, which was whenever I was behind the camera. Here is a poem I wrote last year about myself:

"GREGORY"

Genuine in all that I offer
Reassuring those who lack confidence in themselves
Energized is how I feel when I become thoroughly engaged
Grounded I must stay to keep myself focused

Optimistic even through the toughest situations
Rewarding experiences I bear witness daily
"YEAH" is how I feel after accomplishing a difficult task

What you are about to read will change your mind about acting like a buffoon, or even a chicken with its head cut off, when you have a substitute teacher for one or more days. So, if you think some of what I tell you is farfetched, you are gravely mistaken. This is my story and I'm sticking to it!

Mr. Prosper is the teacher I am referring to. Last year he proved to be the most wonderful and caring substitute teacher I had in any of my classes. Every child living in Cage County, and attending Workaholic Elementary School located on Roundabout Way in Pranksville City, wished for this man when his or her teacher was absent for the day. Every student knew him as Mr. P. and as the nicest, most polite, soft-spoken substitute teacher any of us at this elementary school had ever had in our lifetime. No one ever heard him raise his voice, which was like the whisper of an angel, or even show one ounce of anger. He said "Please" and "Thank you" all the time, and even called students "Mr." or "Miss."

He stood only five feet, four inches tall. This was extremely short for an adult in the eyes of a child, because nearly all the children in grades three to five were either as tall, or even taller than him. In addition to his short stature, Mr. Prosper had the scrawniest muscles I have ever seen on an adult man. He had a hard time lifting even two books—the *Math for Wizards* and *Reading for Bookworms*, which every student, even a seven-year old girl in second grade, could pick up with only one hand.

Every student and teacher thought he was from Pranksville, and that is exactly what he wanted them to think. One day at lunch when I was speaking to Mr. P., he told me that he lived at 1318 Institution Avenue, Apartment 16. I guess he used a third cousin or relative as an undisclosed local address, but I did not ask the details. I'm not sure why he confided this to me.

Weeks later at the computer lab, one of our special classes besides math, reading, social studies, science, and language arts, I wanted to find out more about him, so I did some research. I discovered that he was actually from the tiny town of Nopainnogain, population of about 3,200. In my research, I also located a family photograph. Oh, if only you could see it.

As the youngest of 12 children (six girls and six boys), our fabulous substitute teacher, Mr. Prosper, always ate last. His family dog and cat ate better than he did. Even though his five brothers and six sisters were all taller and stronger, they were neither as smart nor as talented as Mr. Prosper. For what Mr. P. lacked in strength, he had thrice as much in brainpower. He was still smarter than every one of his 11 brothers and sisters put together, plus his mother and father. Some old saying about *the apple not falling far from the tree* was absolutely and most definitely not the case for Mr. Prosper. I would say that he was the *golden apple* of his family.

Nobody ever found out what I discovered about Mr. P. because I did not tell anyone, except for now, because I believe this story about *the best substitute ever* is one that everyone, students, parents, and even teachers, should hear. This is especially true for those mischievous boys and girls that decide to act up, refusing to behave or even attempt to use one ounce of common sense when a substitute teacher is in the room for one or more days. Let this be a fair warning to students who think that a substitute teacher is someone they can take advantage of. You never know what the substitute is capable of!

Chapter 2
School is in Session

SUMMER IS NOW over. The song "This is the Way We Learn New Skills," an elementary chart topper throughout the county, welcomed students back to school on the first day.

"Welcome back students! I am glad to see you back at Workaholic Elementary School! What a wonderful day it is!" exclaimed Principal Paige as she watched her beloved children walk through the front doors and down the right side of the hall in single file to class.

Teachers were either at their doors, or in the hallway, greeting children as they walked by and entered their classrooms, a normal daily morning procedure to ensure a safe, warm, and inviting school environment. Every teacher did this without fail, even if the teacher was a substitute teacher.

Teachers did whatever it took to grab hold of students' attention and to keep each and every single one of them focused on the lesson at hand. Those truly focused encouraged the very few slightly unfocused classmates to get it together, saying that "Learning is FUN!"

Mrs. Fair had a poster in her room of a poem she wrote when she was in elementary school. From a young age, she always wanted to be a teacher.

"WHO AM I?"

Turn Around and Look at Me
Earn Your Points: 1, 2, 3

Answer the Question if You Please
Call for Help if You Need
Hand in Your Work Before You Leave
Evaluate the Problem, Bend of Knee
Return Tomorrow, I'll Never Flee

As the first few months of the school year progressed, between August and October, at the fabulous Workaholic Elementary School, all 417 students both focused and somewhat mischievous, had ZERO days where no one was sent to Principal Paige's office for bad behavior.

This was perfect! It was the *FIRST* record of its kind. *No* other school in the Cage County School District had this record. Inquiring minds wanted to know *how long would it last?* Some thought it could last forever, but nobody spoke about it because they thought that he or she would jinx it, leading to dozens upon countless dozens of puddles of salty tears of sorrow.

Silently, every student including myself thought: take it *one day* at a time, treat *others* how I would want to be treated, do *not* touch anything that does not belong to me, and follow directions the *first* time. If I do this, the record will NEVER fail.

As a kind reminder, one teacher wrote a poem on or about Day 12 of the then current record to help students stay focused.

"WHO AM I?"

Stop Talking
Take Care of Yourself
Understand the Question
Do Your Homework
Enter the Room Quietly
Nonsense is Useless
Turn in Your Work
Stay Focused

Every parent wanted his or her child enrolled at Workaholic Elementary School. In the minds of students and parents it was the ultimate "Best of the Best" elementary school, or in fact, any school, whether it was high school, middle school, or elementary school in the county.

Whenever a student at Workaholic Elementary School left for any sort of reason, there would be a school lottery drawing like NO other lottery drawing for the open seat left behind by the student.

There was great hubbub during the day of the school lottery. Shopkeepers closed their doors hanging a sign saying, "Out to lunch." No police officer could be seen for five square blocks, teachers with a son or daughter enrolled in an elementary school other than Workaholic Elementary called in sick for the day, and a large misplaced hay ball would always carelessly blow in the wind through the center of town. All of the streets would be vacant, just as if it was an abandoned city.

Before I get started, I need to inform you of a few important details. First, our school mascot is the Beaver (**B**ehave as you should, **E**arn respect, **A**nswer questions, **V**alue everything you are given, **E**nter rooms quietly, **R**espect one another).

Second, we have a school song. It goes like this:

"WE ARE THE BEAVERS"

We are the BEAVERS
And we're proud to say
We work hard every day.

BEHAVING as we should
Is as easy as pie
Just by giving a big try.

EARNING respect is top notch
By following the rules
We just don't abuse.

We ANSWER every question
From teacher to us
We answer them without fuss.

We VALUE everything
That is given to us
Sharing it with unending trust.

Quiet as a mouse
We ENTER each room
Leaving no crumbs for a broom.

RESPECTING each other
Is the BEAVER rule
We know that our school RULES!

Nothing can stop us
From getting great grades
Even on rainy days

Workaholic Elementary is where it's at
Being a **BEAVER**
Is _ALL THAT_!

Chapter 3
Steve "The Bee" Sting Arrives

DAY 48 OF *No student being sent to Principal Paige's office* broke the old record by a landslide, and we had no plans of looking back. Neither student nor teacher thought that the streak, just like a winning streak of a professional baseball team, would end. But, then came Day 49 when Steve "The Bee" Sting transferred from Highland Elementary School, located at 345 Cage Square. You see, Steve's mom, Mrs. Sting, had won the school lottery to fill the space of fifth grader, Kaelyn Kadri, also known as "Double K" to his classmates. Kaelyn's mom got a new job in the town of Accelerant in Extinguished City, 25 miles north of Pranksville City.

This school, which sat high atop the hill, had a reputation for students acting in mischievous ways and getting away with only a warning. Teachers would not even bother wasting their paper sending notes home with the mischievous student. Every teacher knew that the note would either not make it home, or if it did, the parent would return it with a side note addressed to the teacher in the child's agenda saying something like "Mr. _____ or Ms. _____, you must be mistaken. I know that my child would not misbehave. Whatever you thought you saw, you were sadly mistaken."

When Kaelyn left, he told best friend, "Hey man, e-mail me about whatever goes on after I move." That friend happened to be Tommy Tacey Tad, one of the most intelligent fifth grade students, also known as "Triple Threat."

Every student at Workaholic Elementary School knew about Steve "The Bee" Sting. He is what any student in his or her right mind would call "The Ultimate Class Clown." Students throughout the county heard through the Highlyprankablevine (the student information hotline) that Steve would do things like poke a student and say, "You just got stung," or he would put a Whoopee cushion on a chair, so when a student sat down it would make "that sound." Steve would even go as far as putting ABC (Already Been Chewed) bubblegum on a seat when a student was not looking.

All of this sounds funny, doesn't it? Well, it is *NOT AT ALL* very funny. How do you think you would feel if it happened to you? Right, that is *exactly* what I thought. No student could learn when Steve would goof off in class. He, she, or even the entire class, would either be laughing so hard they would fall out of their chair crying, or would be so scared that they would be looking over their shoulder every thirteen minutes as if something bad was about to happen to them. It was highly improbable, no, impossible, and there was absolutely *NO* way in the world any student could complete any type of class work. That meant *MORE* homework. And no student I know enjoys doing more homework, do you?

The truth is nobody really knew what Steve would do next, or when, where, or who he would strike. We didn't even bother thinking of *why* he did these things. We just figured that's *just* the way Steve is and it's *just* what he does.

Chapter 4
The School Record Falls

IT WAS THE second hour of school on Day 49 of Workaholic Elementary School's new and growing record. Fifth grade teacher, Mrs. Fair, had finally had enough of Steve's horseplay, and it was only his first day of school.

With the speed of an F3 tornado (measured on the EF Scale), she spun around from the Smart Board (we don't use chalkboards anymore) to stare down "The Bee" as a pitcher does to a batter in a baseball game and pointed her index finger at the door.

Mrs. Fair articulately scolded, "Steve, you are in hot water young man, and that type of behavior will *NOT* be tolerated in *THIS* classroom or at *THIS* school!"

Next, Mrs. Fair firmly instructed Steve, "*GO DIRECTLY* to Principal Paige's office, and *DO NOT* even think about stopping for water!"

My teacher had not seen that type of careless behavior since she taught first grade, which had been 12 years ago. Mrs. Fair was about to have a nervous breakdown, and no, I do *NOT* mean she was going to start breakdancing. She was so horrified at what had just happened she needed to take a break. As she stepped outside of the room into the hallway, she insisted, "Tommy, please take over the day's lesson on double-digit multiplication," a scary subject to us since it was only the third day of the two-week unit.

So, what exactly happened that made Mrs. Fair get so upset? First, Steve woke up late, resulting in his missing the bus, which caused him to request a ride to school from his mother. He was 97 minutes late for class. By that time, backpacks, lunchboxes, homework, sharpened pencils, and paper were all nicely in their places. The class was ready for the day to begin.

Second, math class just started and we had already begun our Daily 10 exercise. All of a sudden, we heard a disturbing *BOOM, BOOM, BOOM* at our nicely decorated door, each one growing louder and louder.

Third, Apple Adams lost her focus, peered through the door sliver of a window from her seat and screamed, "It is Steve 'The Bee' Sting!"

Swoosh! Every single head in the classroom sharply turned to the door's window to see Steve waving with a grin from ear to ear that was so scary the meanest coyote would run back to its mama if it ever saw it.

Even Mrs. Fair turned her head thinking to herself, *here we go!* In her numerous years of teaching, long before any of us students were even born, Mrs. Fair had seen everything, or so she thought. I would say that she was thinking to herself, "What can Steve do that I haven't seen before?"

As Steve Sting walked into class, Mrs. Fair said, "Welcome Steve, I hope you enjoy your time here."

Steve replied, "Thanks Grams." Mrs. Fair's mouth dropped just inches from the floor in disbelief. She pointed to the open seat in front of Cal Cactus and behind Tommy Tad for Steve to sit. Julie Julius sat to his left and Gabby Gabi sat to his right.

All four of them looked at Steve and said, "Good morning, Steve."

Steve answered with a yawn, not even covering his mouth, "Leave me alone!" as he poked Gabby and said, "You just got stung."

Mrs. Fair told Steve to stop as she gave him a pencil and the day's math work. She added, "Next time you do something like that you will be sent to Principal Paige's office."

Steve put his head down refusing to do the work. About five minutes later, as soon as Tommy got up to turn in his Daily 10 work, Steve pulled out the bubblegum he had in the back corner of his mouth and then strategically placed it in the center of Tommy's chair. We call that type of gum, *ABC* bubblegum.

As soon as Tommy sat in his chair he noticed something squishy and sticky on the backside of his brand new light brown khakis. When he attempted to get up, he found himself stuck like glue to bubblegum.

Mrs. Fair heard a little commotion while she was writing on the board. She glanced up at the horizontal mirror above the board and saw exactly what happened. She quickly spun around, faced Steve, and instructed him to go to Principal Paige's office.

With no remorse, Steve hopped up out of his chair, strolled his way to the classroom door like he was some *COOL* kid on television while waving to the class saying, "Catch youse guys later!" He waved one last time as he slung the door open, slamming it as he edged his way to the hallway.

Mrs. Fair opened the door, stuck her head out and yelled down to Steve, "I will be calling your mother!" And after school, she did exactly what she said.

After Steve left the now dismal room, I heard Mrs. Fair take a deep breath and say on her exhale, "Tommy, call home for a new pair of pants, and please look for something in the clothes closet until your mother brings you something fresh to wear."

That was the last straw, or as some would say, the "straw that broke the camel's back," or in this case "The behavior that ruined the school record."

Well, now you know how and why the magnificent school record of "No student being sent to Principal Paige's office" fell. To me, the inappropriate manner in which Steve acted was not the best way for him to make a good first impression here at Workaholic Elementary School. At the conclusion of his journey to the main office, Steve boldly slung open the door to Principal Paige's office. Ms. Inquisitive sat waiting for him in her comfortable cushioned chair, calling his mother as he arrived. Steve's mom was in and out of the office within 15 minutes.

My classmates and I were mighty happy Steve did not come back to class that Friday. I bet Mrs. Fair was exuberant, too.

The rest of that Friday went as smooth as silk. I guess that Principal Paige said something like, "Mr. Sting, I would like for you to take this weekend to think about what you did today, and when you come back Monday, please be on your best behavior. I do not want to see you in my office again."

Chapter 5
Emergency, Substitute Needed

THE NEXT DAY Mrs. Fair got an important phone call from her younger sister, Mrs. Even. She lived in the most *serious* city of Nokiddingaround. She was going to have a baby very soon and needed Mrs. Fair's help. Mrs. Fair told us that the name chosen for the baby was Fortuitous.

Mrs. Fair decided to take 10 school days off so she could visit her sister and new nephew. The following Monday, October 20, Mr. Prosper started the assignment as our substitute for two weeks, (that is 10 school days for those of you who don't know). Every single one of my classmates, yes, even I, jumped as high as possible and happily cheered for joy because we knew that we now had the *best* substitute ever, better that any of us or our friends, or even friends of friends, had ever known.

Day 1

This morning, like many other mornings, I sat on one of the office couches and peered out the window to people watch. My head was like the hands of an old grandfather clock going *tick-tock, tick-tock, tick-tock,* as I witnessed the wonders of the morning outside. My head moved in perfect sync, back and forth, back and forth with the never-ending tic of the dreadful, slow-moving old wall clock. I thought to myself, *why must time move so slowly*, as my fingers annoyingly tapped on the side rail of the couch.

I witnessed car riders waving goodbye to parents as they drove off in their red, blue, green, and black cars, trucks, and minivans into the sunrise. There were students walking to school meeting up with friends coming from different directions by foot and bicycle, and others getting off buses while waving to the bus driver as it pulled away to pick up middle and high school students.

Soon, tired of people watching, I put finishing touches on one of my poems. It is one of my favorites. Try stressing certain words to get a different meaning each time.

"Library Book"

This is a story, all about how
My binding got flipped, turned inside out.
I was snug in my place, right here on the shelf
In between the letters D and F.
Then one day, just about noon
Came a little fifth grader, I don't know whom.
He reached in and grabbed me, squeezed me so tight
He pulled me so fast, I couldn't put up a fight.

I tumbled and twirled as I fell to the ground.
The next thing I knew I was upside down.
Summersaults and cartwheels high in the air
Yelling to the boy, "Hey, this ain't fair!"

Then out of the blue, a familiar voice
"Young man," she said "A book is not a toy.
Come sit with me, and take a look
The importance of holding a book."

All of a sudden, I felt something true.
I was hugged like a baby by you know who.
Out he walked, from here to his class,
Remembering that books are meant to last.

One final request to those who read.
Respect us books is my last plea.
Hug me, carry me, but whatever you do
Don't bend my pages, or I will feel blue.

I am a book, meant to be read
Not thrown like a Frisbee by your brother Ted.
So, when you choose me, please follow this rule
Use a ruler for my place to know where I go.
Follow these rules, and I will be here
For one day, you'll have an itch in your hair.
When you pick me, be careful I beg
And I'll be here, until the end!

Nearly every day I eat breakfast at home and arrive at school early because I ride with my mother who is a second grade teacher here. Today I saw Hailey when I came in. Her mom teaches third grade. She was setting up in the audio/video (a/v) room for her morning routine on the school radio station.

Since my mother did not want me in her room when she was getting ready for the day, I decided to visit Hailey for a few minutes. I knew enough to stay out of her way, so I just watched from a safe distance.

Soon I glanced at my watch and thought, *the early bird catches the worm* as I headed toward my classroom in an attempt to arrive before the rest of my classmates. I sat quietly in the room, seemingly unseen by the others as they entered one by one.

On his first day, Mr. Prosper arrived at school at 7:00 a.m. He took the time to make sure the day's lesson was in order. Sweet Julie Julius arrived early as usual, just like I had, and informed Mr. Prosper about what to expect from Steve.

As she handed Mr. P. the list of character traits that she had created of each student, Julie relayed this message from Mrs. Quest, our librarian: *Mr. Prosper, Hailey is running the school morning show and may be a little late to the morning meeting.*

Apple Adams

She is intelligent, almost on the genius level. Apple sits by Mrs. Fair's desk. I think she will be very famous one day.

Beverly Bacon

Beverly is a wonderful baker for her age, in fact any age, but in class, she is one of the worst complainers. If you can think about it, she complains about it, every little thing possible. Just about every single time we have homework, out comes, "Why do we *have to do* homework?"

Cal Cactus

He is best friends with Tommy Tad. The two of them are always hanging out together. They always work together when Mrs. Fair says we can work in pairs. They are inseparable.

Daisy Daily

Daisy is the daydreamer and follower of the class. She will repeat whatever Beverly says. She is like a mockingbird at times, but everybody likes her.

Eddie Edge

He shouts out his answers and listens to music so extremely loud at home that a person can hear it clearly three blocks away. We think that his shouting is due to trying to talk over his loud music. His mother says he probably will need a hearing aid by the time he turns 30.

Faith Falcon

She has the eyesight that some would even say is like an eagle's, but still likes to wear pretty decorative glasses. Faith loves to read and has probably read the most books in both the school and county.

Gabby Gabi

We call her, "The Gabster." She likes to spread gossip on just about everything she hears.

Gregory Gaines

He's one of the quietest students in this class. Sometimes we hardly know that he is here. He likes to keep to himself.

Hailey Halen

Hailey runs the school radio station. She is up-to-date on every song that airs on the radio. Her friends are Gabby, Julie, Daisy, and Apple.

Ian Idonia

If you have a problem, Ian is the one to see. He is the most qualified mediator of fifth grade. He has a perfect record for solving conflicts between students.

Julie Julius

Julie always arrives early to school. She is willing to help in any way possible. Some say she is a teacher's pet.

Steve "The Bee" Sting

We all know him as "The Ultimate Class Clown." Steve recently arrived here from his old school, Highland Elementary School.

Tommy Tad

He is one of the top five most intelligent students in fifth grade and is best friends with Cal Cactus. Tommy keeps daily detailed notes on what happens at school and e-mails Kaelyn Kadri every day at home.

Upon entering the room, everyone went through the morning routine like clockwork. It included, hanging up book bags, making a lunch choice, handing in homework, writing down the day's homework and special notes, and finally taking a book either out of their desk or from the elaborate classroom library to read quietly until the morning announcements. A regularly scheduled morning meeting followed.

As I was reading one of the books I checked out from the fabulous library, I noticed Mr. Prosper reviewing the class schedule and lesson plans laid out on Mrs. Fair's desk. Shortly after that, I noticed him open a sealed envelope and pull out a letter, probably from Mrs. Fair. Later that day, I asked Mr. P. what the letter was about. He showed me that it was a special note from Mrs. Fair. It read:

Dear Mr. Prosper:

This is a wonderful class. Please let me know on a daily basis what goes on. Please see Mrs. Easel, the teacher next door, to go over the daily work. If there is an assembly or anything special planned, you will receive a message from the front office. Thanks again for subbing!

Mrs. Fair.

Mrs. Fair's Fifth Grade Class Schedule		
Start	End	Class
7:20	8:00	Morning Work and Class Meeting
8:00	8:50	Reading
8:50	9:40	Math
9:40	10:30	ELT (extended learning time) + snack
10:30	11:20	Language Arts
11:20	11:50	Lunch
11:50	12:20	Recess
12:20	1:10	Social Studies/Science
1:10	2:05	Specials (P.E., Art, Computer Lab, Science, Music)
2:05	2:25	Pack up, Reflection, review HW
2:30		Dismissal

When Mr. P. began to take the attendance and the lunch count, I knew that he noticed the special mark by Steve's name. Hailey slipped quietly into the class seconds after the morning announcements concluded, waved to Mr. Prosper and took her seat.

Suddenly, without even an inclination of a warning, everyone, at the same time, glanced around the room at each other and vocalized, "Where is Steve 'The Bee' Sting?"

Tension as thick as the morning fog rolled in and filled the classroom, giving us a vision depth of five inches. Suddenly the classroom telephone sounded off with a thunderous *ring, ring. Ring, ring.* Gabby Gabi just about jumped out of her chair. The entire class busted out laughing, relieving the built-up stress about Steve coming to class. Even Gabby joined in. As we wiped our tears of joy from our faces, our memories regained strength. Our exuberant feeling quickly fell to a below normal level because, Steve "The Bee" was on his way to class.

Who could be calling the class this early in the day? Could it be either Mr. Augment or Mrs. Easel, the other fifth grade teachers? Minds started to wander.

Eddie Edge suddenly remembered, and in frenzy he shouted out the dismal truth, "Oh no, 'The Bee' has not come to class yet."

Silence fell upon us. One could only hear the ping sound of a pin hitting the floor. Facial expressions quickly changed, one by one from the brightest of bright smiles to the gloomiest of sorrowful frowns in fear that it was the office secretary, Ms. Inquisitive, informing Mr. Prosper that Steve Sting was checking in that very moment and would be on his way to class shortly.

"Good morning, Ms. Inquisitive. How may I help you this beautiful morning?" Mr. Prosper joyfully said as he answered the phone.

In her soft, monotone voice, Ms. Inquisitive replied, "Steve Sting's mother just dropped him off. She is checking him in as we speak, and he will be on his way in just a moment."

Mr. P. slowly hung up the phone, faced the still sorrowful class and confirmed our hypothesis by announcing, "Yes indeed class, Steve is on his way."

I heard him whisper to himself, "Am I ready for Steve 'The Bee' Sting?" He quickly rebutted confidently, "I am ready! I have been doing this longer than he's been alive. Nothing can surprise me."

I had a gut feeling I was not the only one that heard him. We, the entire class, wondered exactly the same thing: *Is* Mr. Prosper *truly ready for Steve?*

Time: 8:15 a.m. and reading class has just begun. Anticipation of the regularly delayed arrival of Steve "The Bee" Sting exponentially grew beyond our capable minds as the class and Mr. P. gazed at each other daydreaming of how the day could have gone without Steve.

A split second later, the sound of a knock at the door, softer than usual and a slow turn of the door handle, about the speed of a snail, shocked everyone into reality. Steve "The Bee," also known as "The Ultimate Class Clown," was at the classroom door about to make his grand entrance. Every student, even Mr. Prosper, held his/her breath waiting in anticipation for what was to come.

To our surprise, Steve calmly entered the class, put up his book bag, selected his lunch choice, sharpened his pencils, retrieved his needed supplies for the day, and, as quietly as a mouse, gracefully walked directly to his seat without saying a word.

The first thing out of his mouth was "Good morning, Mr. Prosper, I heard that we were having a substitute today."

Shocked into disbelief, Gabby Gabi could not open her sealed lips to speak a single syllable or mutter a simple word, nor could Faith Falcon believe her perfect eyes. Gabby took out her diary and quickly jotted down what had happened while Faith took off her glasses to clean them, just to make sure she saw what she thought she saw.

Silently I thought to myself, *What's going on? Was* Steve up to something, *or* did he *change for the better?* I had a strong feeling I was not the only one thinking these thoughts.

Reading class came to its end. Soon it was time for math, ELT (Extra Laughter Time for Steve), and writing classes. Surprisingly, the day continued as scheduled, just as any *NORMAL* morning would.

What do I mean by normal? I mean a day like the ones we had while setting the school record here in Cage County where we had no students, and I mean *ZERO* students, being sent to Principal Paige's office. The days before Steve "The Bee" came to Workaholic Elementary.

Steve just seemed to go with the flow, that is, he actually did not act as a class clown like he usually does. Now keep in mind, this is only the beginning of the school day, before lunch and recess. Fresh on the minds of Steve's classmates was the thought, *is* Steve for real? *What* can he be up to?

The old worn out alarm clock let out a loud and disturbing *BUZZ!* That sound gave me the shivers and made me think it was on its last leg. It could croak its last *BUZZ* any day now. Writing class was over.

Beverly Bacon cried out, "Ugh, my hand feels as if it has been slammed in a car door!" As soon as Beverly sounded off, Daisy and Ian chimed in with their complaints.

For the most part, it was TGWIO. This stood for *Thank Goodness Writing Is Over.*

Mr. P. quietly announced, "Class, please line up for lunch. I don't want to be late. I am extremely hungry!"

With no unnecessary cheesy comment from Steve, or anyone else, we all lined up in the straightest, silent line ever witnessed before in Mrs. Fair's class. This was especially true since the arrival of Steve.

In an attempt not to exhibit an excess amazement of Steve's change in behavior, because no student wanted to give him attention he did not need, Mr. Prosper led the class towards the cafeteria, better known to us as Pot Luck Diner.

Earlier, I briefly mentioned the other two fifth grade teachers. Here is a list of their students and a brief description of each.

Mrs. Easel's Class

Kevin Kite

Kevin likes to be called "Kev" for short. He is the Kickball King and is great at just about any sport he plays.

Leslie Lavender

She is one of Valerie's best friends. Wherever Valerie goes, Leslie follows. Even best friends need their own space sometimes.

Melony Marbles

She is as tough as any of the boys. Melony really does not like playing with dolls. Some of the boys are scared of playing against her in fear of losing to a girl.

Nancy Nelly

She is one of the quietest students I know. Nancy loves to read and is at the top of the school's reading list.

Oscar O'Malley

He is one of the best soccer and kickball players at any of the elementary schools in this county. Oscar is good at any sport he plays, just like Kevin.

Pete Perturbs

He has short blond hair, wears glasses, and loves to read any genre of book. He is not what I would call well-coordinated and is clumsy at sports.

Quade Quinn

Quade is a math whiz. He can do any single or double digit multiplication problem in his head. He even has a head start on division.

Randy Rhymes

He is the science guy. Randy loves learning anything that has to do with any type of science.

Urquhart Urbane

He speaks with some sort of accent. His friends call him "Hart." He always brings his lunch because he despises school food. I do not know too much about him.

Valerie Victors

Valerie is the beauty queen of the class. Every guy has a crush on her and she knows it. Some of the girls say she has some boys do her homework.

Wayne Warrick

He fills in as the coach during any 'class versus class' competition. Wayne carries a whistle at recess every day.

Xavier Xanto

He is one of the tough guys. Xavier is friends with Oscar. In this class, the two of them are always seen together.

Yancey Yikes

Yancey is short, skinny, and clumsy. He is not very good at any sport he plays. Just like Pete, he should be more of a spectator.

Zachary Zander

He likes to be called "Zac" for short. Zac is one of the most popular boys in the school. Even the teachers think he is a cool guy.

Mr. Augment's Class

Alice Zabrina

She is one of the brightest students in the fifth grade. Some say she will be in advanced classes in middle school.

Brian Yonder

Brian's father was a jet pilot in the Air Force. The summer after Brian's first grade year, his father received a TDY (Temporary Duty Assignment) in southern California. Before the big move, his dad requested that Principal Paige hold a spot in the fifth grade for Brian. He knew when the assignment would end. Every now and then, Brian tells us about his time in California.

Cedric Xarles

Nearly every day during recess, Cedric is around Brian, becoming totally intrigued by the stories he tells about moving around the country and what it was like having a father as a jet pilot. From these stories, Cedric decided he wanted to be a jet fighter pilot when he grew up.

Devin Wonders

She is the food eating champion of the fifth grade. Yes, I did say 'she.' Her challengers should not have allowed her size fool them; they lost every time they did.

Edgar Valliant

All of the girls here call Edgar a "true gentleman" because he always holds the door open for the girls and the women teachers. Edgar is the only student in fifth grade who wears a collared shirt with a tie to school every day.

Francis Underwood

Don't let his last name fool you. He is the tallest boy in fifth grade. He can just about slam dunk the basketball. Every boy wants him on his team. Some of the girls think Francis is some sort of dream. What does that mean?

Gail Tanner

She is the best singer in the entire fifth grade. All of the girls want to be as good a singer as she is. Gail has won more school talent competitions than anybody else put together.

Hue Sanders

He is the most talented artist of any student in the school. Hue has been drawing since he could hold a spoon and can draw anything asked of him. Sometimes when he has time, he helps our art teacher, Mrs. Mastery.

Isabel Ramos

Crafting is her forte. She can create amazing things. Her projects always look the best. Just about all the girls want to work with her to decorate projects.

Jennifer Quizzer

She is at the top of any social studies class in fifth grade. Jennifer can tell you anything you want to know about South America, Africa, and Australia.

Kellie Paolo

Page after page has been turned in for each writing assignment she has been given since second grade. Even though Kellie was not in my class this year, I still heard about her from my friends after school.

Liona Odessa

If any student in fifth grade has a question regarding science, he/she goes to Liona. We all want to be in her group during science class. Although great in academics, she's not so talented in sports.

Marty Nielson

He runs any type of betting; no teacher knows about it. The only thing wagered was our snack. This would be paid off the next day if we lost, or we would receive an extra snack if we won. A few students almost got caught sneaking the snack to recess. This led to the exchange of snacks after school, a for-sure way of *not* getting caught.

Chapter 6
To the Cafeteria

Day 1 (continued)

WE WALKED DOWN the main hallway without the slightest squeak of a shoe or the sniffle of a runny nose. About halfway to Pot Luck Diner, Principal Paige stopped us to give her highest praise, "Job well done class! Keep up the fantastic work!" Her positive recognition left us with the feeling of walking on air as we proudly walked with our chests sticking out and our heads held up as high as kites. That exuberant feeling ended as soon as we got wind of *that smell.*

Weeks before Steve arrived at my school I wrote and entered a poem in a poetry contest. It was about the school cafeteria, and it goes like this:

"That Smell"

Down the hall there is a smell
My nose twitches here and there
All day long, it hangs around
Driving me crazy, without a sound

My friend Joe, he stumped his toe
Rushing around, to and fro
Sally yells, "What can it be
This fabulous smell that's bothering me?"

Reading is over, I could hardly focus
Because that smell, was driving me loco
We line up, and open the door
To the hallway we go, in an orderly flow

Stronger it grows, the closer we get
Little Sally Sue, about threw a fit
Aromas are clearer, I know that smell
It's nothing but the lunchroom air

Of course, the poem by no means describes the cafeteria here at Workaholic Elementary. The sweet, no, the hair-raising smell, of Pot Luck Diner along with the gooey, squishy-squirting sound of the hand sanitizer machine brought us down to Earth as we cleaned our now dirty-sweaty hands from our intense classwork.

Before reaching for the sweetest tasting carton of strawberry milk, and the blinding golden food tray layered with cheese stuffed-crust pepperoni pizza, carrots, and chocolate pudding, I noticed Tommy secretly gazing at Steve.

Steve's cheeks continued to get redder than a red fire truck zooming by to put out a blazing five o'clock fire. His chest poked out with pride such as that of a gorilla pounding on its chest saying, "Hear me! Look at me!"

Tommy whispered to me, "What is Steve thinking? Is he up to something?"

I just gave Tommy *that eye*; you know, the one a guy silently gives his friend to confirm, *I'm thinking the exact same thing!*

With his left hand, Tommy reached for his tray filled with chicken nuggets, sauce, carrots, banana, and a wiggly-wobbly, lime-green sugary treat. In his right hand, he held his carton of the chocolatiest of chocolate milks, which will keep any student who drinks it vibrantly jumping with joy, higher than a professional pogo stick jumper could, or run as fast as Olympic gold winner, Speedster Sound-Barrier, but only until the end of recess.

Tommy's gut feeling about Steve being up to something was about to be confirmed. Just after I took a huge bite out of my cheese stuffed-crust pepperoni pizza, I saw Tommy about to dip his golden-crispy chicken nugget into his sweet honey mustard sauce while staring at it with the intent to devour it.

Steve was last in line. I did not know what he got until he sat down. As soon as the chicken nugget covered with sweet honey mustard sauce touched Tommy's tongue, "The Bee" stood up and yelled, "Food Fight!" as he slung his lime-green treat in the air, hitting poor Pete Perturbs square in the middle of his glasses.

Embarrassed at what had just occurred, Pete grabbed a handful of carrots and intensely threw them back at Steve with the blazing speed of a major league pitcher, but with the accuracy of a blindfolded chimpanzee, nailing Zesty Zane in her hair, striking Yancey Yikes in both arms, and grazing Wayne Wakes in his left leg.

Steve was ducking and dodging food from all directions with the agility of the world famous contortionist, Jimmy "Slim Jim" Jones.

In a sarcastic tone, Steve retaliated by yelling, "You couldn't hit the broadside of a barn!"

All of sudden, a thunderous, ear-piercing voice rang out clear as day over the loudspeaker.

Then, we all froze in place like well-sculpted statues. No one made a sound or moved a muscle. "*DROP* WHATEVER *YOU* HAVE IN *YOUR* HANDS!" demanded Principal Paige, in the harshest voice we have ever heard and with the sternest look, which would make even the toughest and meanest criminal locked up in jail for life cry like a little baby.

A loud *thud* sent a deafening echo throughout the room as every single piece of food from every grimy hand and finger fell to the now grotesque cafeteria floor. It was arranged in such a way that even a vicious junkyard dog would turn its nose up at it.

Surprisingly, if you could see it from the ceiling, you would think that it was a famous piece of abstract art. However, neither teachers nor lunch-room staff felt that way.

Principal Paige's face turned fire-engine red. She was so furious that I thought I saw steam coming out of her ears as she asked, "Who initiated this?"

Steve stood in the middle of the cafeteria with hardly a piece of food on him while every fifth grade student, the only grade involved in the first ever food fight at Workaholic Elementary School, pointed his and her colorful finger directly at him.

My educated guess was Steve felt as if he had the lead role of an actor on stage with the spotlight on him, while his ear to ear devilish grin had returned. Steve "The Bee" was back to his old self. Teachers, notified of the commotion, quickly arrived and gathered students, leaving the cafeteria in its now unique state.

If you are worried about the involved students, they all ended up okay. Clothing was wiped clean and the majority stayed at school. A few students had clean clothes brought to school. We went to recess to run off that steam built up in the cafeteria. If I remember correctly, teachers gave us an extended recess, which does not happen very often. When we got back to class, there was not very much time to do our social studies lesson, so Mr. Prosper allowed us to read and talk quietly with our friends before we went to specials. We went to the computer lab that day.

The lab teacher, Ms. Defragmenter, knew everything about anything there was to know about computers. This was no ordinary class. Instead of just being hooked up to some program, working on math facts and reading, we engaged ourselves in matters such as researching topics that personally meant something, learning different languages, and learning how to type correctly.

Steve went nowhere! He stayed frozen in his spot, dead in the middle of the mess, or work of art if you look at it from a different point of view, until Principal Paige handed him a pair of gloves and an apron to put over his clothes.

She pointed to the trashcans and firmly instructed, "Your consequence is to clean this *entire* cafeteria *by yourself*! Get the attention of someone here in the cafeteria if you need anything. Do you understand me?"

Still frozen, Steve nodded *yes* several times with a glazed look on his face.

Principal Paige added, "After cleaning up this mess, return to my office ASAP (As Soon As Possible.) You and I are going to have a little one-on-one chat about what I expect out of my students here at Workaholic Elementary School."

As soon as she left the cafeteria, Steve snapped out of his trance-like state and began cleaning. His armpits soon became covered with the slippery, sloppy, grimy mess he created as he pressed down into one of the filled-to-the-brim trashcans. Moments later, just like a crazy man, he mumbled to himself, "That was *great!*" Quickly answering too, "Yes, *yes*, it was. Need to be *sneakier* about it next time."

Oh, what would it be like to be a fly on the wall? I would be able to see Steve get what he deserved with the multiple eyes I would have, instead of the few one-eyed cameras scattered around the room. However, I could not take the risk of possibly having him swat me because of my being nosey, curious as I would call it. Any sane person would think Steve was insane if they saw what he was doing.

Several questions raced through my mind at the same time. I wondered, did Steve *really* learn his lesson, *how seriously* will he take his one-on-one talk with Principal Paige, and *can* or *will* he ever learn his lesson?

Amazingly, the cafeteria was spotless after only one hour and eleven minutes of Steve's labor-intensive consequence. How do I know how long it took him to clean up and what he said when he was talking to himself? At the end of the day, I reviewed the security tape on one of the extra monitors before I went home. I just had to know. Oh yeah, by the way, I can also read lips.

After throwing away his grimy gloves, he handed the food-filled apron to Mrs. Servings, the head cafeteria woman of Pot Luck Diner, and then he leisurely strolled out into the hallway as if he had no cares in the world.

Keep in mind the extremely important appointment Steve had with Principal Paige that day. Everyone at school knew she did not like it when any of her scheduled appointments were late. Hence, being late was *NOT* in his best interest, but at that moment Steve was not taking anything at all very seriously.

This was Steve's second time in the office this year. Ms. Inquisitive said, "Steve, please sit down and I will inform Principal Paige you are ready to see her."

Sitting down calmly, he began to whistle a tune, "Doom, da, da, Doom, da, da, Doom, Doom, Doom, Doom, Doom," which he had heard somewhere before. I had heard the same tune before myself. It foretells when something *bad* or *horrific* was about to happen.

Ms. Inquisitive looked up from her work for a moment and saw Steve giving a short smirk. My best guess was that she was silently thinking *boy, he does NOT know what he's in for.*

The quick turn of the doorknob and swift opening of the office door startled Steve, raising his heartbeat by 23 beats. As he placed his hand over his chest, he could feel his heart about to come out of it. There, standing in the doorframe of her office, with her arms crossed and a stern look only an upset mother could give, Principal Paige said, "I will see you now, Mr. Sting." Now, allow me to remind you that this is Steve's **second** time in Principal Paige's office.

Slowly and carefully, Steve got up from his chair and walked in with his head hung down low, just like he or any person his age might, like if his dog had just died. Steve knew that Principal Paige was upset that he took his time getting to her office after cleaning the cafeteria and that he was the student who had started the food fight. Deep down, I think he did *NOT* really care that he was in trouble.

Steve did not return to class that day. Principal Paige called his mother to come pick him up. Since Steve finished his consequence of cleaning the cafeteria for starting the food fight, Principal Paige decided to allow Steve to come to school the next day.

Now that I think about it, I do recall that Ms. Inquisitive secretly stated, "As my eyes followed Steve into the principal's office, I *saw* his usual grin as he held his head down low." She added, "I believe he was putting on an acting job for Principal Paige, and it seemed to work."

Neither students nor teachers will ever know the exact content of the discussion in the office that day, except for Principal Paige and Steve "The Bee" Sting.

At the end of the day, Principal Paige told Mr. Prosper, "I had a one-on-one talk with Steve today, and he will be on his best behavior the rest of the year, especially the rest of the time you are here." She concluded, "If he is any trouble send him to my office, and I will take care of him for you."

Chapter 7
Post Food Fight—Perhaps a New Steve

Day 2

THIS DAY, MY classmates and I noticed something strangely different about Steve. At recess, I spoke to Cal, Eddie, Ian, and Tommy. We concurred on our hypothesis; something truly *was* going on with Steve "The Bee" Sting.

Earlier that day during reading, math, ELT, language arts, and even during lunch, Steve actually acted like a normal student at Workaholic Elementary School.

Cal stated, "I am totally serious! I can't believe he actually turned in *all* of his work. I don't know if it was completed or not, but the fact is, he actually did something he was supposed to do."

Eddie added, "Oh yeah, he even kept his hands and feet to himself when we were in line going to lunch. Wow, he didn't even horseplay one bit!"

Even though Ian had a perfect record as a mediator in the fifth grade, there were a few days, far and in between, when he got stuck, became dumfounded. His level of confusion at the time shockingly surprised my friends and me.

Ian admitted, "Guys, I'm in a great hubbub about Steve. I could not believe my eyes when I witnessed the numerous times he raised his hand to answer a question."

Just as Mr. Prosper blew his whistle ending recess, Tommy whispered, "It is incredible he has not even attempted to poke anyone or say 'You just got stung' either."

Our amazement continued through social studies. We were so focused on the lesson that Steve and his possible antics never crossed our minds. Perhaps this really was a new Steve.

Art class was next. As I lined up, I remembered Steve had not been to art class. I thought for a second, will he continue doing what's *right*, or convert back to his *old ways*? Guess what? He behaved like a perfect student.

On our way out the door, Mrs. Mastery, the art teacher, commented to Mr. Prosper, "Steve was a fabulous student. He followed my directions perfectly. You must be happy to have him in your class."

Mr. Prosper smiled extra big and said, "Thank you very much, Mrs. Mastery. Steve has been such a delightful addition to our class. Have a nice day."

When we arrived back to class, Mr. P. was still smiling as he jotted down his notes from each class about how Steve was doing and how the rest of the class reacted. At the end of the day he showed them to Principal Paige. More than likely, with best intentions, they felt Steve was indeed making forward progress.

The day after the food fight was Day 1 of setting a new school record of *Zero Students Being Sent to Principal Paige's Office*. The question in the minds of the entire school was, "How long will **this** record last? Will we beat our first record of 49 days?"

To emphasize such a tremendous feat for Steve, as well as the class, Mr. Prosper created a table on the dry erase board representing the correlation between the days he substituted for Mrs. Fair to the number of days of the new record. Of course, the record included the whole school.

I thought it was a brilliant way of showing the class the past and probable future. The question mark on Day 2 showed us what could be, and we all knew what that was—a new record of zero students being sent to Principal Paige's office.

Day 1	Food Fight
Day 2	Start of New Streak (Day 1) YES
Day 3	Continuing Streak (Day 2)?
Day 4	
Day 5	
Day 6	
Day 7	
Day 8	
Day 9	
Day 10	

Chapter 8
Moving in the Right Direction

Day 3

THIS DAY OF school with Steve was another magnificent, fabulous, and stupendous day. Workaholic Elementary was on its way to continuing its streak for the new school record of no student being sent to Principal Paige's office. I heard a few stories floating around during recess; there had been a couple of close calls, but students quickly realized they needed to regroup and refocus. This supposedly happened in second grade, but everything seemed to work itself out. Even the fourth graders stayed focused.

Just a little tidbit from me before going on with the tale about Mr. Prosper, the best substitute teacher ever.

I remember last year; fourth grade was a tough year for my friends and me. Even the most diligent boy or girl in fourth grade had problem days where extra help was needed to stay focused, even if it was from a substitute teacher. Like it or not, it is part of growing up, and guess what? Teachers, yes even yours and mine, went through roughly the same problems. So, if you think that regular teachers, substitute teachers, or any other adult at school does not understand you, think again. The answer might just surprise you, if you just ask.

Steve continued to amaze everyone. Even though he was 15 minutes tardy to class, Steve answered every comprehension question after reading the assigned tale in "Stories for Fifth Graders," completed his assignment sheet of double-digit multiplication, wrote on the day's topic, "I am going to be _____ for Halloween," and answered questions during social studies. Steve was introduced to Coach T. during P.E. Anything Coach said, Steve did.

Before we left, Mr. Prosper briefly spoke to us about having goals, both short-term and long-term. Before the end of the day announcements, he stated, "Boys and girls, your assignment is to tell me your goals by writing about whom, and/or what you want to be when you grow up."

A few answers rang out as loud as Principal Paige's voice blasted out over the intercom.

Mr. P. added, "Take this home with you and show your parents. This is the theme for the fifth graders during the Fall Festival. If you have any questions, please refer to the handout about the festivity."

Before he gave us this assignment, Mr. P. filled in one cell on the table, but nobody except me paid any attention.

Day 1	Food Fight
Day 2	Start of New Streak (Day 1) YES
Day 3	Continuing Streak (Day 2) YES
Day 4	
Day 5	
Day 6	
Day 7	
Day 8	
Day 9	
Day 10	

After the last bus drove off and parents picked up their children, Mr. Prosper wrote his daily note about Steve to Mrs. Fair and spoke to Principal Paige. I had a good inclination that Mr. Prosper was excited to write something positive about Steve again.

Something was weighing on my mind at that time, and I believed it possible to be in the back of the minds of Mr. Prosper and Principal Paige. That irritating thing racing through my mind was that *either Steve turned over a new leaf,* meaning he saw his bad ways only got him into trouble, or *he was playing possum,* which in his case meant his old ways were not dead, but there was a high probability he was up to something.

Numerous pondering minds throughout the school wanted to know what Steve was going to do next. Having attended Workaholic Elementary School since I was in Kindergarten, and now just about to complete the first half of the fifth grade, I knew each and every day was going to be an adventure. Even in the fifth grade, we children, students if you prefer, could have off days along with our good, fabulous, and super star days as well. These so called, OFF days happen just as much to us as they do to the younger ones when we get off track, but we all quickly refocus with a little assistance. Like it or not, it is all part of growing up.

Nevertheless, the question about the possibility of Steve *continuing to amaze us* or *reverting back to his old ways* remained on the minds of everybody at school. Whether or not we wanted to admit it, we all thought it at least one time or another during the day.

Only time would tell, and at that time it was still too close to the day of the first, and hopefully only, food fight started by Steve "The Bee" Sting. We, the student body along with teachers, staff, and administrators, could only take it day-by-day. For those of you readers who want it to be more specific, it actually was second-by-second, hour-by-hour, class-by-class, and finally, day-by-day.

Chapter 9

Recess

Day 4

FOR A LITTLE inspiration, to see how we would react, Mr. P. added a question mark beside Day 3 of the current record of zero students being sent to Principal Paige's office. This important table on the dry erase board was created with his favorite red Write-On marker to illustrate the days he had been substituting for Mrs. Fair. It actually had been on the board since Day 2, but none of us paid any special attention to it.

Day 1	Food Fight
Day 2	Start of New Streak (Day 1) YES
Day 3	Continuing Streak (Day 2) YES
Day 4	Continuing Streak (Day 3)?
Day 5	
Day 6	
Day 7	
Day 8	
Day 9	
Day 10	

Classmates trickled in slowly but surely. As I sat in my seat quietly doing my own morning work, I witnessed each one going through his or her daily motions, much like a worker on an assembly line. The morning work assigned for the day consisted of correcting sentences and reading comprehension. Finally, the rest of the class noticed the table Mr. Prosper created.

"What is that table for, Mr. Prosper?" Cal Cactus inquired.

With no delay, Mr. Prosper replied, "That is a great question, Mr. Cactus," then followed up by calmly announcing, "Class, please stop what you are doing so I can explain what I drew on the board. This table represents each day of my substituting compared to the streak of the school record."

As soon as Mr. P. explained what the table represented, Steve walked into class. I thought to myself, *wow*, he's *not* tardy.

Seconds after arriving to class, the tardy bell rang, *Do, Re, Mi, Re, Do.*

Milliseconds later, concluding the chimes' end, our principal joyfully announced over the intercom, "Good morning boys and girls. Today is Day 3 of our new, never-ending streak! Let's keep the record going where none of you fine, brilliant, and fantastic students are sent to my office. Keep up the fantastic work, and have a *BEAVER* of a day!"

Narrowly escaping being tardy, Steve sat down and began his morning work just as Mr. P. softly called, "Class, please join me down in the front of the room for our morning meeting. If you have not completed your morning work, it can be completed during recess."

Without the slightest sound of disgust, Steve calmly rose from his chair, pushed it in without slamming it into his desk as he usually did, and joined the class.

Sitting tall in the reading chair, not even slouching one degree, Mr. P. announced, "Today we will pass around our mascot, Busy Beaver. Whoever has our mascot may share something. You may say 'Pass' if you do not have anything you would like to share."

Not to bore you with all the details, we mainly shared which TV shows we watched the previous night, what trick(s) our pet did, how far we were able to get on one of our favorite video games, and what movie was coming out on the weekend, which we planned to watch.

When Steve, the only one I will tell you about, had his turn, he talked about how his team, the Wasps, was going to win the football game this Saturday. He was only able to say, "We are going to wipe ..." before he was interrupted by the new timer Mr. P. had set before the meeting. He was probably going to say, "We are going to wipe the floor with them!"

The tiny red and black device sounded off with a parrot-like voice that said, "Time is up, move along; time is up, move along," letting us know that morning meeting was now over, and it was time for the awesome subject of reading.

Some of us probably thought to ourselves, *thank goodness* the bell *saved* us from hearing the *boring* details of Steve's football team.

While making our way to our seats, Steve made the uncanny comment, "Arr. Timer wants a cracker?" We could not help ourselves but to giggle.

Mr. Prosper looked up at us from Mrs. Fair's desk and replied, "Class, let's *thank* Steve for the morning joke. Laughter is good for the body."

In perfect sync and harmony, we shouted "Thanks, Steve!" We did it in our indoor voices, of course.

With a slight crack of a smile in the corner of his mouth, in which his dimples could barely be seen due to his head being buried in his desk searching for his reading book, Steve answered, "You're *welcome*, you guys. Mighty *glad* I could help."

I don't *quite* know why, perhaps it was the way Steve gave us his reply; it sent a shiver down my spine.

Later on that day, at recess, while talking to Tommy and Faith, I asked, "Either of you pick up on something the way Steve said 'Mighty *glad* I could help' this morning?"

Tommy scratched his curly red hair and insisted, "No man. I'm sorry, but I didn't notice anything."

Faith gracefully rearranged her glasses and added, "Gregory, I agree with Tommy. I did not notice anything either."

While we were having our little chat I noticed Steve was playing tetherball, and Pete Perturbs was in line waiting to challenge him. Steve was able to finish his morning work just after completing the assignment in writing class so he could play at recess.

If you remember, Steve landed one of his hurling shots of food on Pete during the food fight. I'll bet anybody 10 pieces of candy from Halloween that Pete is planning some sort of payback on the court against Steve.

Faith and Tommy both went their separate ways as I stood to the side of an unused four square part of the flat top of the playground. Steve had won three games in a row, and Pete was next in line. Yancey Yikes stepped into the challenger's area. He shook like bacon, hiked up his corduroy pants, and gave a reassuring node to Steve that he was ready, just as a major league pitcher gives to his catcher verifying the signal that a fastball is coming.

The booming sound of Steve hitting the ball sounded like Kevin Kite, also known as the "Kickball King," kicking a grand slam in the final match of a best-of-three game series. Yancey was so shocked by the sound and the speed of the ball coming directly toward his head, he ducked as the ball wrapped around the pole for the first time, just about slipping and falling on his buttocks.

Sorry to inform you, but Yancey did not have enough time to recover from his near fall to stop the tetherball from wrapping around the pole for the second, third, and fourth time, resulting in a fourth straight victory for Steve.

By his time to play, Pete had enough time to study each of Steve's wins over his victims. Surprisingly, Steve was a good sport and shook the hand of each challenger at the end of each match.I don't know if he was being a good sportsman, or just being a little arrogant.

Pete strategically placed one foot in front of the other as he stepped into his spot in the 360 degree circle. He planted his feet firmly on the cement with a slight bend in his knees. In a cool manner, Pete slowly pulled his blue glasses case from the back pocket of his blue jeans, and in the most precise manner, he removed the sunglasses attachment and clipped it to his glasses, making the slightest *click* sound, which two magnets make when their two opposite poles are connected.

From his other back pocket, Pete pulled out a small grey plastic tube of hair gel. He was able to hold it and open it with one hand. After squirting just a little bit in his other hand, Pete recapped the tube with the same hand and put it back in the same back pocket.

Next, he gently rubbed the gel in his hands, and then slicked back his hair until it was pointy like a porcupine.

Finally, Pete was ready to face Steve "The Bee" Sting, mano a mano (man to man, or in this case student to student).

Since Steve was the current champion for the day, now on a four game winning streak, it was his honor to serve. Steve shouted, "I am the *King* of the tetherball court! I am *unbeatable!*" in the most obnoxious voice I have ever heard from a student.

This out of the ordinary voice echoed throughout the playground. Everyone stopped what they were doing and focused their eyes on Steve to see what was going on. When they saw that it was only "The Bee," they returned to what they were doing.

Steve even had the audacity to follow up with a cackle, "Ha, ha, ha, ha, ha! Little Pete, you will be my number *five* victim."

I knew that somebody, perhaps a teacher or two, must have been picking up on something here about Steve's behavior. Maybe it was just my imagination running wild. I don't know.

With his hair slicked back, sunglasses on, and Pete Perturbs standing firm in his *ready* position, Steve "The Bee" was given the signal to serve.

As the ball glided swiftly through the air, it made a *swoosh* sound from the contact of Steve's massive closed fist. Since he didn't want to lose, he added a little extra to this serve. It was the hardest hit he could manage.

Steve turned his back to Pete as soon as he served the ball, just as he had done against his previous challengers. Since Steve's serves were so massive, he had absolutely no reason to believe Pete would have even the slightest chance of returning it.

To Steve's surprise, Pete leaped high up in the air with his arm soaring above his head and his fist clinched tight. With his timing just right, Pete gave the firmly padded tetherball a smashing hit that echoed throughout the playground, even louder than Steve's obnoxious chant.

Before Steve knew it, he saw the ball out of the corner of his eye flying back to him at lightning speed. Sadly, he was too late to either block it, or time his massive swinging fist with enough force to hit the ball back to Pete.

The crowd gathered closer and closer to perhaps witness a tetherball match for the ages. Even the teachers became filled with curiosity. They were becoming witness to the outcome of a spectacular match.

"One!" the crowd shouted as soon as the ball wrapped around the pole the first time. We all noticed Steve's face becoming a little pink. As soon as we excitedly yelled, "One!" the ball was wrapping around the pole in Pete's favor for the second time. Next, a little louder, and with more glee, we yelled, "Two!"

Faster and faster the ball gathered speed as Pete hit it. Those of us right around the match got so much into the game that every single student on the playground, even those who did not play this game of tetherball, gathered around the initial spectators and joined in the chant. Louder and louder the chanting grew: "Pete, Pete, Pete, Pete, Pete, Pete."

Steve's face grew redder and redder with each chant.

No matter how Steve tried, he could not touch the ball. Pete stared down the ball ready to hit it again as it glided over Steve's head. Pete nailed the ball, *BAM!* He hit the ball right smack dab in its sweet spot with his fist of furry. As he did this, the crowd screamed, "Three!" as the rope rapidly twirled around the pole for the third time.

Steve was panting like a dog in need of a large bowl of ice cold water. Pete, the prime contender, was wearing out the present champion. A second later, the ball was traveling so fast it may have been even less than a second; the crowd joyfully screamed, "Four!"

That was it! Pete Perturbs was the new tetherball champion for the day. He had beaten the day's reigning four-time champion, Steve "The Bee" Sting.

Pete put out his hand for Steve to shake, and to my surprise Steve shook it. Right after the handshake, a whistle blew to end recess.

On our way to line up in our class lines, I made an extra effort to stand close to Pete. I wanted to be sure I was one of the first students to congratulate him on his victory. I asked, "Pete, how do you feel after what some would call, 'The match of our age'?"

With a look in his eye I have not seen since we started school together in Kindergarten, Pete replied, "I feel like I am on top of the world."

He then motioned to me he had something important to say. Pete waved for me to come closer and said, "I have to tell you something about Steve," as he looked around to make sure Steve was nowhere near.

"What is it, man?" I replied.

Rubbing his hand, Pete calmly whispered, "Man, after shaking hands with Steve my hand still hurts. It's still a little numb. Oh yeah, I think he is furious I beat him so easily. Keep an eye on him the rest of the day, will yah?"

"Pete Perturbs, please get in line," Mrs. Easel requested, followed by, "Oh, by the way, very nice game."

Wiping the sweat from his head with the back of his hand, Pete replied with a smile, "Thank you, Mrs. Easel. It was a difficult match, but worth the challenge!"

Mr. Prosper lead our class directly behind Pete's class. As soon as we entered the school, Mr. Early, the science and social studies teacher, who comes into Mrs. Fair's class once a week said, "Excuse me, Mr. Prosper, Ms. Inquisitive has requested your presence in the office."

Standing in front of the line with his right hand held up high in a quiet manner, Mr. Prosper got our attention. "Class, I am needed in the office. Mr. Early will take you to class and lead the lesson. Please be on your best behavior."

Now wait a minute, you *don't* expect me to tell you why Mr. P. was called to the office, do you? Well, I *can't* tell you. What I can tell you is that I had a keen eye on Steve as Pete requested. If Steve even so much as made a twitch in the wrong direction, or I felt that he was up to something, I would be the first, or at least one of the first, to know about it. My 'Steve' sensors were now tuned in.

Mr. Early, like all the other teachers here at Workaholic Elementary, always held high expectations for his students, and I expected nothing less.

I do not think you have met Mr. Early yet. He stands as tall as a professional basketball player, has muscles as big as a professional football player, and he is as fast as a pro soccer player chasing 30 yards after and catching his opponent with the ball. One day he told me that in high school he ran track and played on both the football and basketball teams. As a boy, he also played soccer.

Well, that's enough information about Mr. Early. As we walked to the room, I noticed him keeping an eye on us through the reflection in the windows we passed.

As I glanced in the next window myself, I noticed Steve ever so slyly inching his left hand closer and closer to pinch Apple in her side.

He did not do this just once. *NO*, he dared to do it three times! The first time he did it, Apple kindly said, "Please stop, Steve."

Steve said nothing in reply; he just smiled. About seven steps later, Steve did it again.

In reaction, and with a slight rise in her voice, Apple insisted, "Steve, that's enough. Stop bothering me!"

It was to no avail because Steve just kept on smiling, not even noticing that he was being watched by Mr. Early, who saw everything.

Just two doors down from our room, Steve again had the nerve to think about pinching Apple in her side for a whopping third time. By that time, she had reached her boiling point. Apple's instinct that something was about to happen kicked in the exact moment Steve motioned toward her side.

Before Steve's hand got less than halfway to pinching Apple, she turned around and firmly scolded him in an even louder voice, one that you could say was almost at a playground level.

Apple insisted, "Stop *pinching* me, Steve, before *I* hit you!"

At last, we had finally reached our room. Mr. Early and I locked eyes as I passed him in the doorway heading toward my seat. I believe that I knew what he knew and vice versa.

Just as Steve, the last one to find his way to his seat because he was lollygagging around, sat down, Mr. Early kindly placed a piece of paper on his desk and whispered into Steve's ear, "Steve, this is your consequence for your actions in the hallway. I know what you did to Apple."

Steve looked at Mr. Early, smiled, and with his left hand, he spread his fingers out wide, and slapped the piece of paper that had been placed on his desk. A loud *WHACK* echoed in the room.

Steve then wadded up the piece of paper into a little ball and made a hook shot into the trashcan from his seat. He neither bothered to place it, nor aim for the recycle box. We have a state recognized recycling program here at Workaholic Elementary School.

Mr. Early did not utter one single word to Steve. He just nonchalantly walked over to Mrs. Fair's desk and wrote out a note.

Next, he announced, "Students, follow the instructions on the dry erase board and answer the questions independently. I am available if anyone needs help."

Chapter 10
What's Next?

Day 4 (continued)

A LOUD, THUNDEROUS *boom, boom, boom* knock at the door startled us. We had just begun our assignment again after being interrupted by Steve's wadding up the paper and unnecessarily making a hook shot with it into the trashcan.

The visitor could be seen through the sliver of glass that was the classroom door window. When Mr. Early motioned the person to come in, I glanced up briefly thinking it was just another teacher here to see Mr. Early. A few seconds later I lifted my eyes up for a second time while thinking of an answer to a question. That second look at the visitor turned into more of a stare.

Not a sound could be heard, not even the gasping exhale of a breath of someone with a cold. Silence filled the room, yes, even Steve, at least for the moment. None of us could believe our eyes.

I took a quick glance around the room without moving my head even a fraction of an inch. We were stunned into silence. Every head was looking directly at the visitor standing in the front of the class.

The man had an extremely large amount of muscle. He was even wearing tights, just like professional wrestlers wear on TV. His were camouflage, the pattern of what someone in the military would wear. For a little extra bite to his character, he wore a mask.

The visitor announced in a harsh and raspy voice, "Good morning class. My name is Pick-on People Punisher."

Still in disbelief at what was taking place, "Good morning, Mr. Triple P.," trickled out of our mouths in a calm, monotone manner.

"Thank you for the respect students, you can call me Triple P. or P. to the Third Power," he replied in his deep, raspy voice as he peered around the room from left to right and back from right to left to get a good look at us. I felt as if he was sizing us up.

The next thing to come out of his rather humongous mouth was, "I hear we have someone in this class that likes to pick on other students." Every single finger pointed at Steve.

Triple P. strolled to Steve's desk. He leaned in as close as possible and uttered, "Okay, so you are the young man who likes to say 'You just got stung.' You even gave yourself the nickname 'The Bee,' didn't you?"

Leaning way back in his chair with his eyes closed and hands clasped behind his head, like relaxing in a hammock in spring, Steve replied in a rather confident manner, "Yep, that's me!"

I could see the veins bursting out of both the Punisher's arms and neck. In reply to Steve's arrogance, Triple P. proclaimed, "Well, I have bad news for you, *Mr.* Bee! Today, we are going to have ourselves what I like to call an *intervention*. That means you and I are going to have a little bit of fun. Or, at least *I* will!"

Judging by the vague look on Steve's face, he was not at all taking Triple P. seriously. He was probably thinking that man *doesn't* scare me! I am 'The Bee,' and *nobody* gets one over on me!

Before Steve could finish his daydream of a thought, his desk shook like a Level five on the Richter magnitude scale. Steve fell out of his seat shaking from the event.

Steve did not open his eyes immediately. I guess he truly was deep in thought, or perhaps he thought that he was still dreaming. However, after opening his eyes, Steve found himself in a unique situation; he was lying flat on his back on the classroom floor.

We, the entire class, laughed so hard that quite a few of us started to cry, resulting in some of us falling out of our seats.

"Stop laughing at me!" Steve yelled in frustration as he pushed himself up to a seated position on the floor.

None of us took him very seriously at that moment. I heard a few hecklers say, "It looks like 'The Bee' just got his *stinger* taken away!"

He randomly pointed at students saying, "I'm going to get you! You had better watch your back! You will get stung! Nobody laughs at 'The Bee.'"

Watching from a near distance, Mr. Early jotted some additional notes down on Mrs. Fair's desk for Mr. Prosper. I could only imagine what he wrote.

Finally, Steve picked himself up off the floor and brushed off his clothes with his back toward Triple P.

No sooner than he did, Triple P. loudly grunted, "About-face! That means, turn around soldier and face me!"

Steve nonchalantly turned around in a rather saddened-slouched position. "Stand up straight, son! Have some pride in yourself!" ordered Triple P.

In amazement, Steve stood straight up at attention, with his arms down at his sides ready for his next order.

Triple P. added, "Now, march yourself to the front of the class. Left, left, left, right, left. And, halt."

A few of us gawked at what we saw. Steve was marching to the front of the room like a soldier. He actually followed the orders *to the letter* without giving any lip.

That amazement came to an abrupt end after Steve took a few extra steps followed by a turn away from Triple P. I believe that Steve did it on purpose.

Without the slightest hesitation, Triple P., known as the "Punisher" to Steve, commanded, "That means *STOP*, soldier!"

Startled by the even louder and harsher tone in the Punisher's voice, Steve froze in his place. I did not see even *one* little insignificant muscle flinch.

Steve again had his back to Triple P. and now faced Mr. Early, who was still standing by Mrs. Fair's desk. Neither a smile nor a frown was seen on this teacher's face. I would call it a *poker face* because he probably did not want Steve to see any type of reaction from the way he was behaving, or the way the Triple P. was confronting Steve's behavior.

The next thing Steve heard was Triple P. commanding, "Steve, turn around and face the class!"

Finally realizing Triple P. meant business, Steve followed this order and awaited the next one to be given, which was "At ease, soldier!" This meant stand up straight with hands clasped behind the back and don't move.

Next, Triple P. inquired, "Class, who here has been picked on by Steve?"

Knowing that they had protection, Gabby, Tommy, and Apple's hands shot up in the air like rockets roaring high in the sky.

"Well now, Steve, it seems like you have a tremendous problem of keeping your hands to yourself," insisted Triple P.

Steve nodded, "yes" in a silent reply as he faced the class.

Triple P. then turned to face the class in a precise manner and requested, "May I have the three students who raised his or her hand form a line in the center of the class?"

Gabby, Tommy, and Apple quickly formed a single line and awaited further instructions.

Next, the Punisher faced the accused and inquired, "Steve, what do you need to tell your classmates?"

Instantly, Steve replied in an apologetic tone, "I am sorry for my actions," as he lowered his head in shame.

Triple P. thanked Steve for his initial apology and then insisted, "Steve, I would like for you to shake hands with Gabby, Tommy, and Apple, and apologize personally to each one of them."

One at a time, Gabby, Tommy, and Apple stood in front of Steve, looked him in his eyes, and shook his hand.

Steve followed each handshake with what seemed to be an even more sincere, "I apologize for my actions. It will not happen again."

At the conclusion of the handshaking, Mr. Early sincerely complimented, "Steve, job well done, young man."

Before the Punisher stepped one foot out of the classroom door, Mr. Early recovered the wadded up paper Steve had thrown into the trash can and said, "P. to the Third Power, since Steve apologized rather well, how do you feel about you and I suspending this writing consequence I hold in my hand?"

Triple P. verified, "That is a fabulous idea, Mr. Early. I concur with your decision. May I borrow the paper for a moment, please?"

With a gentle hand signal, Triple P. motioned for Steve to come see him, leaned close to his ear, and spoke in a calmer tone than before, probably to make sure Steve understood the deal about to be made.

Luckily I was close enough to hear Triple P. say, "Steve, your consequence of writing this sentence 25 times has been suspended. That means it has been taken away. However, if you choose to repeat anything you have done in the past or do anything new in the future against school rules, then the initial consequence of 25 times will be reinstated, plus an additional 25 times for each independent poor behavior. Do you understand?"

Steve inhaled slowly through his nose and exhaled even slower through his mouth while nodding "yes." Steve held out his hand, looked the Punisher straight in the eyes, and in an assured tone replied, "P. to the Third Power, we have a deal!" while giving him a firm handshake.

Triple P., the Punisher, or P. to the Third Power, whichever one you prefer, saluted as he left the class announcing, "Thank you for your cooperation. I will return if another situation occurs. So *please* be on your best behavior, *or …*"

We sat silently in our chairs without saying a word to each other. Staring at the clock, time seemed to stand still. The final three minutes of social studies class ended abruptly. Wow, how time flies when you are engaged. We had music for specials that day.

This was one of the best transitions to line up to leave the class we have ever had. It was quiet. I mean not a peep was heard; probably due to the shock from what had just occurred. Seconds after Mr. Early opened the door to let us out into the hallway, Mr. Prosper arrived and greeted him.

In a delightful manner, Mr. Prosper graciously shook his hand while saying, "Thank you, Mr. Early, for taking care of the class for me. I will take it from here. Would you like to join us on our way to music?"

Mr. Early sincerely declined, "Thank you kindly, Mr. Prosper, but I have some papers to grade and lesson plans to review in my room."

None of us mentioned to Mr. Prosper what happened in class while he was out. The only thing on our minds was going to music for our special. Mr. Chord, our music teacher was teaching us some new songs. We lined up in rows according to our voice range.

Now, don't get me wrong, most boys my age still think they can sing, but they are sorely mistaken. Most of our voices are changing, and without proper training, our voices sound like off-key baying hounds. While we warmed up our voices, I thought I heard Steve belt out a couple of *WOW* notes, sounds I have not heard from a fifth grader's voice in a long time. By the way Mr. Chord looked at Steve, I believe he thought the same, but for some reason did not say anything to him.

Oh, Mr. Prosper filled in information for Day 4 on the table as the dismissal bell rang, and said, "Class, great job ending the day on a good note. We are continuing our streak. Keep up the fantastic work, and have a nice day."

Day 1	Food Fight
Day 2	Start of New Streak (Day 1) YES
Day 3	Continuing Streak (Day 2) YES
Day 4	Continuing Streak (Day 3) YES
Day 5	
Day 6	
Day 7	
Day 8	
Day 9	
Day 10	

Chapter 11

The Competition

Day 5

THE FIRST THING I saw when I walked into class was the table Mr. P. had created to remind us of our behavior while Mrs. Fair had been away.

Day 1	Food Fight
Day 2	Start of New Streak (Day 1) YES
Day 3	Continuing Streak (Day 2) YES
Day 4	Continuing Streak (Day 3) YES
Day 5	Continuing Streak (Day 4)?
Day 6	
Day 7	
Day 8	
Day 9	
Day 10	

I was impressed at the record Steve had set for himself. Since the day after the food fight, Steve had managed to stay in class for three consecutive days. I hoped today would be Day four.

Yesterday was a *close call* or *narrow miss,* if you prefer. If it had not been for the Punisher visiting us, Steve surely would have been sent to Principal Paige's office.

Again, Steve was able to make it to class before the tardy bell. He sat calmly as Faith shared, "My father and I went to the mall yesterday to get me a new pair of glasses. Yeah, I know I don't have a prescription, but aren't these frames just fabulous? We got ice cream after that."

Eddie shared during the morning meeting. "I saw my doctor yesterday to check my hearing. The doctor said I need to turn my music volume level down from a seven to a three if I want to save my hearing."

We all noticed Steve was exhibiting self-pride by the way he walked in line in the hallway and completed his work. His behavior was nearly perfect. Steve did not try any of his antics, old or new!

Even though Triple P. seemed to make a positive impact on Steve, some students, such as Ian and I, continued to wonder if Steve was *just going through his daily motions* to hide some ultimate, *devilish-pranktifying* scheme he would unleash on the class or school.

We thought this because we all knew that "The Bee" was the "Ultimate Class Clown," and sometimes the *BEST* clowning or prank comes after a long rest.

I don't think the agreed increased writing consequence with the Punisher would defer Steve from setting one of his plans into action, even with two or three extra days added to the initial consequence.

Sitting on the ground with pencil, paper, and clipboard in hand during recess probably would give Steve more time to contemplate a plan while writing. Only time would tell.

The only near confrontation on Day five was during math class. Here, Steve and Tommy got into it by raising their voices to a level so high that the rest of us had difficulty concentrating on our assignment. We decided there was no other choice but to watch in anticipation to see what would happen next.

At the climax of the pandemonium, Mr. Augment came running into our class from across the hall. He flung open the door so fast it scared us half to death. He hollered, "What are you two boys yelling about? I could hear you clearly across the hall. I thought there was a fight."

Mr. Prosper was sitting in the chair in a reclined position with his hands behind his head with a nice, shiny smile on his face. He knew one hundred percent that there was nothing bad going on. "Mr. Augment, thank you for your concern. These young gentlemen are simply having an intense conversation, although it be rather loud. It is about who is the best and quickest at double digit multiplication."

Mr. Augment replied, "All right Mr. Prosper, if you say so. Have a nice day. And please, can you ask the two fine young gentlemen to keep their voices down?"

"Yes, sir, you can count on me," Mr. Prosper quickly answered, concluding with, "Have a nice day!" as Mr. Augment closed the classroom door.

It had all started during the beginning of the lesson completing our review of ten double-digit multiplication problems on the board. About five minutes into it, Steve whispered to Tommy, "Hey Tommy, I bet you your chocolate milk I can answer all the problems correctly before you can."

"I'll take that bet, Baby Bee!" Tommy quickly replied as he glanced back at Steve, giving him the *evil eye*.

"Hey, stop looking at my paper!" Steve yelled at Tommy.

"I'm not looking at your paper, Steve, so stop trying to get me into trouble. I do not need to copy you. I am smarter than you!"

Steve angrily rebutted, "Are you calling me stupid, Tommy? If you are, you better watch your back!"

Calmly, Tommy told Steve, "No, Steve, I am not calling you stupid. Please, stay focused and quiet down so we can finish this bet and see who really has the fastest pencil."

I glanced up at the timer on the desk. It was about to go off, 5, 4, 3, 2 ... In perfect synch, Tommy and Steve turned their bodies, placed their right foot out into the isle with the left to follow, got out of their seats, and raced to the front of the room to claim victory for completing the morning work first.

If you asked me, I would have called it a tie, at least the race to the front of the room. The rest of the class was briefly sidetracked from all the commotion leading to many of them being unable to complete the problems.

Mr. Prosper announced, "Class, time is up. Please put your pencils down. Today, I will allow you to grade your own paper."

Following a brief catch of breath, Mr. Prosper continued, "Ah, it seems that we have two volunteers already up front to go over the problems. Tommy and Steve, please write ..."

Both boys turned around lightning fast, quickly grabbed the closest dry-erase marker, and then wrote the problem so fast, Mr. P. did not have a chance to finish his sentence.

Seconds later, after completion of the first problem, Mr. Prosper caressed his chin with his right hand resting on his left arm, letting out a slight, "hmm" as he reviewed both answers.

Both Tommy and Steve were dying in anticipation of Mr. Prosper's verification that his answer was correct and the other's was not.

In his rather peculiar voice, Mr. Prosper enthusiastically remarked, "Fantastic job! Boys, both of you successfully answered the question."

"Can we stay up here and do the rest of the problems?" Steve asked in his most kind and soft tone.

It was a rather *begging* manner, I would say, nothing of which I have heard from him at any time before.

"Well, I don't have a problem with it. Class, what do you say?" asked Mr. P.

I know that I wanted to see these two face off, and I am glad the rest of the class agreed by the shout of their unanimous, "Yes!"

One by one, each question was answered with extreme diligence from both Tommy and Steve, and Mr. P. would go through his usual and predictable "hmmm" as he reviewed each answer.

A tally mark here and a tally mark there. Wow, there was a tie. Steve is more intelligent than I thought, and probably the rest of the class agreed with me. The T-chart was now even at nine tally marks on each side. Problem 10 took the longest amount of time. It gave both Tommy and Steve a little bit of trouble.

Every eye beamed a hole directly through the two competitors as they neared completion of the final problem. At last, what seemed to be forever to me, the competition concluded.

Anticipation filled the room as Mr. P. *AGAIN* let out his "hmmm" *while* tediously reviewing the final answer from both boys. Nervous fingers tapping on desks sounded off in perfect harmony to the tune of "I'm Smarter than You Are!"

Under his breath, I barely heard him say, "Uh-huh. Yep. Yes sir. By golly, I believe so!" Next, in one of the most excited voices I can remember hearing from him, Mr. Prosper joyfully announced, "Congratulations boys, both of you got all 10 problems correct. Boys and girls, we have a tie at 10 correct answers each!"

Amazingly, Steve turned to face Tommy, held out his hand, and gave a firm handshake while saying, "Nice job, Tommy. You were a great opponent. Next time I *will* finish before you. I can't wait until *we* meet again!"

While Tommy firmly shook Steve's hand, he gleamingly smiled while staring directly into Steve's eyes and rebutted, "Next time I will feel more inclined to de-sting 'The Bee.'"

If I didn't know better, I could have sworn that I bore witness to the *supposed to be nice handshake* turn into a *handshake of muscle*. Both hands grew from a pale tone to light pink, ending in fire engine red as Tommy and Steve stared each other down.

Mr. Prosper saw he had to intervene before Steve and Tommy took their little showdown to the next level.

They were snapped back to reality when Mr. Prosper kindly interrupted, "All right, boys, that's enough. Go back to your seats, please, so we can continue our math lesson."

Besides that little squabble between the two math whizzes, Tommy and Steve, nothing worth mentioning happened on Day five (Day four of the new streak). At the end of the day, Mr. P. filled in the table on the board so we could have visual confirmation that the school streak continued on in a positive manner.

Day 1	Food Fight
Day 2	Start of New Streak (Day 1) YES
Day 3	Continuing Streak (Day 2) YES
Day 4	Continuing Streak (Day 3) YES
Day 5	Continuing Steak (Day 4) YES
Day 6	
Day 7	
Day 8	
Day 9	
Day 10	

Chapter 12
The Race

Day 6

THIS DAY SEEMED to begin as normal as the others. Mr. P. arrived for day six of his ten day substituting assignment. Some of us realized that Mrs. Fair had been out for six days, but felt fine because we had the best substitute ever.

Day 1	Food Fight
Day 2	Start of New Streak (Day 1) YES
Day 3	Continuing Streak (Day 2) YES
Day 4	Continuing Streak (Day 3) YES
Day 5	Continuing Streak (Day 4) YES
Day 6	Continuing Streak (Day 5)?
Day 7	
Day 8	
Day 9	
Day 10	

Shockingly, on the morning of Day six, which was a very chilly morning, Steve arrived at school earlier than ever. Mr. Prosper could not believe his eyes and neither could Gabby Gabi, known as the "Gabster," if I have not told you already. Of course, the next thing I noticed was Gabby writing down a special note in her "Little Pink Book." It had to be something about Steve showing up to class on time.

This was the third day Steve participated in the class Morning Meeting. Sitting quietly in my spot hoping he would not talk about his football team *again*, I pondered the question, *what will Steve say this time when Busy Beaver is passed around?*

When it was his turn to share, Steve held the mascot in his left hand while he slowly lifted his right pant leg with his right hand to show off his new shoes. "Guys, these are my brand spanking new shoes, which my mother bought for me yesterday after school."

Ian raised his hand and asked, "What kind of shoes are they?"

As calmly as he possibly could, due to his hand quivering, Steve replied, "These are the new, fresh, hot off the shelf Nimblers."

After a few oohs and aahs from a few of us, Steve stressed how the salesperson told him, "They are the only running shoes now available that can make anyone wearing them run as fast as lightning can strike the ground from high up in the clouds."

Before passing Busy Beaver to the next person, Tommy muttered, "Steve, I challenge you to a race during recess."

With pride, Steve rebutted, "I accept that challenge, Tommy. You can't beat me!"

Milliseconds after accepting the challenge, Daisy added, "I challenge you too, Steve!"

In perfect harmony, Steve and Tommy replied, "You can't race us because you are a girl. This is a race between us boys."

Retaliating, Daisy sassily said, "What? Are you two *boys* afraid of losing to a *girl?*"

With eyes wide open, Tommy and Steve frantically shook their heads from left to right, simultaneously whimpering, "No. No. We're not afraid of a girl." Steve and Tommy each took a deep breath to regain his confidence. In unison, they agreed, "Okay! You got it! You can race us." The challenge had been set.

For a twist on things, the morning meeting had ended on a challenge, Gabby rushing out of the room grabbing the restroom pass, and Mr. P.

saying, "Please hurry back." Every class before lunch went fine, nothing worth mentioning. The race was the only thing on all of our minds.

The news of the day's first ever of its kind challenge traveled quite quickly through the student Highlyprankablevine. On our way down the hall to eat lunch, all I could think about was the race, and as soon as Mr. P. set foot in the cafeteria, there was complete silence.

Every single eye was burning a narrow hole directly through the three competitors. Slowly, the lunchroom prattle started back at each table. I only noticed a little bit of chatter at the two tables closest to the lunch line. Of course, the conversation was all about the race.

I attempted to eat my lunch in silence while struggling to tune out the noise and confusion in the now boisterous cafeteria. I found myself day-dreaming about the possible outcomes of the race. I didn't even get a chance to complete all the possible outcomes or finish my lunch before it was time for my class to go to recess. Tommy, Steve, and Daisy were the last to dump their trays and the last three in line.

I was second in line. As soon as the door opened, I hurried as quickly as possible, securely holding my camera in one hand, to take my place to watch the race, making sure I was one of the first in my class to secure a spot.

Third grade classes and below had already gone inside. Fourth graders interested in the race were awaiting the fifth graders to come out to begin the race. My theory about word of the race getting around school was proven true when I noticed there were more students than normal standing around the flat part of the grassy area we used for races.

Both boys and girls were standing shoulder to shoulder. Instead of being at the front of the race, I had to take my place at the end, which was directly on the finish line.

I thought to myself, *perhaps* being at the *end* of the race on the finish line would be a much better spot for me than being at the beginning. Setting up at the finish line would allow me to take pictures of the entire race.

As I do every morning before I come to school, I checked the day's weather. According to the weatherperson on the television, the day's temp-erature would be about 75 degrees around recess time. And this was one of the few times she was right. Luckily, for us, the slight breeze flowing through the air made it feel not quite so hot.

Anxiety filled the air as we waited for the three competitors to arrive for this first ever type of race at Workaholic Elementary School. Finally, after my nerves had just about reached their boiling point, I witnessed the three highly motivated competitors strolling to the starting line as if they had no cares in the world, at least for recess. It seemed like they were walking in slow motion as the light breeze blew through Daisy's hair.

The level of the screaming and hollering as Tommy, Steve, and Daisy approached the race area was so loud I thought I was about to lose my hearing. I covered my ears to block out most of the noise. Suddenly, I remembered to check a side pocket on my camera case. Luckily, I had remembered to pack my earplugs. When I am at a place with an extremely high level of noise, I use them so I can get into my zone. I take better pictures when I am there.

Sometimes, like that day, the noise level would be so high that the earplugs did not work as well as they usually did. Thank goodness for Wayne Warrick from Mrs. Easel's class. He had his trusty shiny whistle. I believe he, too, had become irritated by the hubbub. Slowly, Wayne reached under his collared shirt and took hold of his whistle. He calls it "No Mas," which means, *no more*. Wayne took a deep breath and blew as hard as he could. Every student around him stopped dead in his or her tracks and looked at him thinking, *what? Sorry!* I *will* be quiet now!

The student in charge of any type of betting, kept on the *hush-hush*, was Marty Nielson from Mr. Augment's class. This meant that *zero students* ever told a single teacher about the betting at school. Of course, the only wagers we ever made were on things like ice cream money ($.50), or our snack from school or home. No teacher has ever found out, so if you even think about it or do tell one of them this, I will deny ever knowing you, and I will *plead the fifth* when asked the question.

With Melony Marbles from Mrs. Easel's class at the starting line, Marty running the bets on the sidelines, and I, Gregory Gaines, ready for a photo finish, the race was set to start.

Ian stepped in front of the three racers and dragged his left shoe through the dirt to make a starting line while Nancy Nelly from Mrs. Easel's class scraped the ground to make the finish line.

Melony, Marty, and I looked at each other as soon as the lines were drawn and gave a slight nod to give the *OK* to start the race.

The runners took their mark as Melony waved, motioning them to get ready. Steve was on the outer left side, Tommy was on the outer right side, and Daisy was square in the middle.

Melony eloquently reached in her back left pocket with her perfectly painted bright pink fingernails and pulled out a bright yellow and pink-hearted handkerchief. She slowly raised it high above her head. Finally she yelled, "On your mark! Get set! Go!" Her handkerchief floated to the ground like a feather after she yelled "GO!"

The racers were about a quarter of the way down the track by the time the handkerchief had finished falling to the ground.

For the first few seconds it was neck and neck. All of a sudden, Tommy took the lead, all the while giving the *evil eye* to Steve saying, "Hey, Steve, you can't catch me!"

Digging deeper within, Steve was able to find that little extra boost he needed to pass Tommy. He replied, "Not so fast, Tommy! See *you* at the finish line!"

I was so busy focusing on what Tommy and Steve were doing and saying to each other that I forgot all about Daisy. I was amazed she was able to keep up with the two boys.

Seconds from the three racers crossing the finish line, I knelt down in a ready position on the smooth, silky, green grass. I embraced my trusty camera with my left hand and used my right hand to zoom in and out. I had set it for fast moving objects, so I would be able to take multiple shots in a row. I wanted to make sure there was only one undisputed champion.

At first, both eyes were glued to the tiny viewing screen of my camera, but the sun just happened to be shining in the right spot, the wrong one for me. I pressed the button quickly to change from the viewing screen to going old fashioned by using the optical view finder (the tiny hole on the top left backside of the camera) and then reattached my right index finger back to the shutter button. My superior peripheral vision caught a glimpse of the three racers inching closer and closer with every step.

Immediately, my brain sent the message to my finger to press and hold down the shutter button. The only thing I heard was *click-click, click-click* ten times, all the time blocking out the distracting screaming from the spectators.

I took a long and slow inhale through my nose and exhaled even slower through my now parched mouth in relief, thinking, *finally*, the race is *over!*

As I stood up from my crouched position, setting my camera to view the forty pictures I took, I noticed each racer holding up his and her hands in the air in victory just feet from the finish line. I was silently thinking, *oh my, what* is going on?

I scanned through the pictures one by one, flicking back and forth between the last three pictures. I hollered, "Hey guys, come over here! You are not going to believe your eyes!" when I knew that there was obviously an indisputable winner.

Every spectator quickly huddled around me, hurrying, wanting to take their turn to see the pictures while Daisy, Steve, and Tommy stood off to the side, hands clasped together on top of their heads catching their breath from the intense race.

Through all of the mumbling around me, I know I heard Tommy and Steve still going at it about which of them was the winner, not even considering Daisy as a threat.

After scrolling back and forth through the pictures slowly several times, and playing them fast like a movie while every student was hanging around waiting for an answer, I saw, without a doubt, who the winner of the race was.

Marty cleared his throat and announced in a loud and boisterous voice, "Boys and girls of Workaholic Elementary School, today we have witnessed a race like none other ever before seen here."

"Come on! Get on with it! Who won the race?" chanted Brian Yonder.

"Calm down, Brian, and don't get your undies in a bunch," Marty quickly rebuked.

Like announcing the first place winners on one of those award shows, Marty used his balled up fist as a microphone and boldly pronounced, "The winner, by a nose, is Daisy!"

The air now filled with pandemonium as students lifted Daisy on their shoulders and carried her to the blacktop chanting, "Daisy! Daisy! Daisy!"

Tommy followed behind the crowd waiting his turn to congratulate her on her victory.

Poor little Steve was still at the finish line. I saw him on his knees, clasping his hands together yelling with his head tilted up to the sky, "Why? How can it be that a girl beat me? I don't lose to girls in anything." Finally, he bent his head in defeat, stood up, and slowly made his way to join the crowd.

The voice of a true sportsperson, Tommy, said, "Congratulations, Daisy, you are one of the fastest runners I know." And he shook her hand.

"Thank you, Tommy. That is a mighty nice compliment from a true sportsman," Daisy replied as she shook Tommy's hand.

Daisy must have shaken about thirty hands or more and said "thank you" twice as much before Steve was able to say something.

As Steve stepped up to the plate, he slowly raised his head from the bowed position he had been holding it in because of the disgust and shame he felt from losing to a girl. At last, Steve stirred up enough courage to make eye to eye contact with Daisy.

Daisy could see how upset Steve was as he approached her. Just as he opened his mouth to offer his congratulations while holding out his right hand, she kindly interrupted, and in the sweetest voice I've heard from any girl in the fifth grade, Daisy shook Steve's hand and said, "Steve, you are a fabulous runner. Maybe next time we can compete against each other, just you and me."

In a dumfounded look, truly surprised to see Daisy not rubbing in her victory over two of the fastest boys in fifth grade, Steve graciously accepted her kindness and the offer of a challenge in the near future. He smiled while shaking her hand saying "Great race, Daisy. It was too close for comfort. Next time, I will be more ready for you."

The rest of the day went on without a hitch. Every now and then, I heard some student saying something like "Great race, Daisy!" or "Glad you kicked those boys' butts!" or "Way to go, girl!" or even a girl raising her fist in the air saying "Girl power!"

Steve did not focus on what was going on around him. He just continued through the day as if the race did not even happen. That was proved even more in the computer lab during specials. While I was doing some research on the history of the camera and photography, I noticed Steve doing research on running. I'll bet anybody their chocolate milk that Steve was doing whatever it took to be ready for the next time he raced against Daisy. The main thing on his mind was probably *there is no way that I am going to lose to a girl again!*

I don't know if I saw pep in his step or what, but Steve seemed a little happier than he had been since he transferred here.

The end of the day arrived before I knew it. Mr. Prosper filled in Day six on the board with a smile on his face and commented, "Class, here ends Day six on a good note. Let's conclude tomorrow on another good note and add another day to the continuing streak. I know none of you wants to go to Principal Paige's office."

Day 1	Food Fight
Day 2	Start of New Streak (Day 1) YES
Day 3	Continuing Streak (Day 2) YES
Day 4	Continuing Streak (Day 3) YES
Day 5	Continuing Streak (Day 4) YES
Day 6	Continuing Streak (Day 5) YES
Day 7	
Day 8	
Day 9	
Day 10	

Chapter 13
We're Going to P.E.!

Day 7

AS I ENTERED the classroom I momentarily thought, *boy oh boy, what a way to start the week!* Sitting in my seat I silently continued, *that* race was *something* yesterday! I had a good feeling it was on everyone's mind. I just hoped nobody mentioned it when Steve was around. We surly did not want to make him upset in any way because we all knew what he could do when he got upset.

Milliseconds later, Steve walked into class as I softly whispered, "Well, speaking of the devil." It's a good thing that Steve did not hear me, because I didn't want to be the one student who assisted him in doing something to break our new school record.

I kept my head down low and my mouth closed while I completed my morning assignment, just like everyone else. I neither wanted to make eye contact with Steve, nor did I want to have a target on my back by taking a chance of upsetting him, so I just kept my thoughts and comments to myself. I wanted to remain invisible to Steve today more so than any other day he had been here, and I am positively sure the rest of the class felt the same, especially Daisy.

Today, during reading class, we had a post-test over what we had learned the past couple of weeks. The entire class was silent, and each of us put up laminated manila folders on our desks as privacy boarders. Upon completion of our tests, we silently read books. I took a quick sneak peek above my privacy boarder to see if anyone was looking at Steve, and just as I thought, nobody dared to do so.

We did not hear one single peep out of Steve during math class or even during ELT. Steve pretty much just kept to himself. Oddly enough, he was quiet as a mouse. Not one time did he show a gleam in his eye giving the notion that he was about to do something.

He even amazed us during writing class when he maintained full concentration while writing on the topic "If I had a time machine, I would ..."

I saw him turn in three full pages in perfect cursive. I only had one-and-one-half pages saying, "I would travel back in time to see the Wright brother's first airplane flight."

At lunch, Steve sat at the corner of one of the lunch tables all by himself. We thought he wanted some alone time, so we gave it to him.

Recess was the same. Steve sat against the wall away from everyone, just staring into the sky and smiling. Nobody paid any attention to him because they were too busy having fun playing.

Seemingly in some type of feel-good trance, Steve raised himself off the ground and took his place in line; he was last in line to go back to class for social studies.

I can't recall exactly who it was that I heard, but I know it was a boy from another class who whispered, "This is not normal for Steve, for him to have his lips zipped."

In Steve's favor, Gabby replied, "I say that he is a perfectly normal student doing exactly what one is expected to do, so keep your comments to yourself!"

Shortly before art class, while sitting at my desk, I looked at my watch and thought, *come on*! It *can't* be! It's been nearly *six hours*, and Steve has been *THIS* perfect. *What* is going on? Am I *dreaming*, or is this *some nightmare*?

At the conclusion of that scary thought, Mr. Prosper announced, "Class, time to line up for art class. Kindly line up in a straight and silent line."

Without fail, we did exactly what he requested of us, even Steve.

Shortly before we entered the hallway, the phone rang. As Mr. P. swiftly walked toward the phone, he whispered, "Oh my goodness, who can it be now?" The name in the caller ID window was Ms. Inquisitive. In a joyful manner he answered, "Good afternoon, Ms. Inquisitive, how may I help you?"

Ms. Inquisitive relayed the message to Mr. P. He told us verbatim, "Mr. Prosper, I have an important message to give you. Mrs. Mastery will not be in today. She is sick. We could not get a substitute for her, so you will be going to P.E. with Coach Tough."

Immediate pandemonium filled the room as we all cheered and hollered. I like art class, but please do not get me wrong, every student in elementary school, including me, *LOVES* to have P.E. over any other special class.

Before we realized it, Mr. P. was standing in front of the class with his right hand raised and his left index finger over his closed lips telling us, "Please give me your attention and be quiet."

The entire class snapped back to reality, immediately stopped talking, and got back into our straight line. We then proceeded to P.E. without stopping.

Mr. Augment's class was already lined up just outside the gym because it was their usual day to have P.E. Mr. Tough, (we call him Coach T.) motioned to my class as soon as the last student from Mr. Augment's class entered the gym. Every student silently marched directly to his or her assigned spot and patiently waited for Coach T. to make his announcement.

A few whispers filled the air, but nothing too loud for P.E. As soon as Coach stood in front of both classes not a sound could be heard. At the top of his lungs, Coach T. hollered, "Boys and girls, are you ready to have some FUN?"

A very low, almost unanimous, "Yes" could barely be heard.

Coach hollered at the top of his lungs, "Boys and girls, I can't hear you! I said *do you want to have some FUN?*"

Immediately after his last syllable, a total and unanimous "**YES!**" was shouted at the top of our lungs and echoed throughout the gym for a few seconds.

Coach Tough replied, "Great! Today we are going to play a game of Beaver Ball."

I, along with everyone else, shot both of our hands high up in the air from our seated position in excitement with a stupendous, "Yeah!"

For those of you who have never played it before, it is a version of dodge ball, except there is only *ONE* ultimate winner. It can be a quick game, or it can take all class.

Beaver Ball Rules

1. One to three balls can be used.
2. A thrown ball can hit any body part of the target except for the head.
3. A thrown ball can be ducked, dodged, hopped over, and blocked with a held ball.
4. Once you are hit, you must exit the game.
5. If the person that knocked you out of the game is hit, therefore out of the game, then you may reenter the game.
6. Rule 5 means that a player must keep an eagle eye on the game, especially on the player who took him/her out of the game.
7. Players exit and reenter the game until there is only one player left.
8. The last player is the one who has been fortunate enough to take every other player out of the game.

A few years ago, somebody wrote a little song, poem if you will, and it goes like this:

"BEAVER BALL"

Balls flying and bouncing
While children are dodging, ducking, and jumping
Someone got hit, "Ouch that hurt!"
Yelled at the player, "Just wait, you will see!"
To the sideline some go
Return later to play
Throw the ball again
To hit back the foe
Time will only tell

If one winner will be

Crowned as King or Queen today

Just play and see

After Coach's little speech, he blew his whistle and we scattered from our spots like birds on a tree branch flying off in different directions after hearing a deafening loud *boom-boom*, from an old car backfiring.

Coach T. held in his hands green, red, and yellow high-bounce dodge balls. One by one he rolled each one in a different direction. Every scaredy-cat student, except for three brave boys, Brian Yonder and Cedric Xarles from Mr. Augment's class, and Eddie Edge from Mrs. Fair's class, ran straight towards the rolling balls, while the rest of us ran around the gym like chickens with our heads cut off.

Brian Yonder crouched down, hoisted the green ball from its rolling position, and then immediately turned to the right to locate and nail Jennifer Quizzer on her left leg.

While she hobbled to the sideline, Cedric gathered the yellow ball with great momentum and successfully grazed Cal Cactus on his shoulder and Beverly Bacon on her left foot. It was a two-for-one shot!

Steve thought he could hide in the far corner of the gymnasium while everybody else ran around. Eddie Edge, one of the best players of the game, saw this as he took hold of the red ball. Eddie scooped it up with his right hand, ran full speed, and hurled the ball, nailing Steve dead center in his chest.

Steve rubbed the spot on his chest where he was hit. On his way to the sideline, Steve stared down Eddie as they locked eyes, such as a professional football player does after being hit by an opponent.

Balls ricocheted off of students in a high velocity manner. Very few balls were caught. Every student who was legally hit by a ball, and therefore out of the game, waited patiently on the sideline in anticipation that the student who knocked him/her out of the game got knocked out of it, too. This meant a second chance and time to reenter the game, have fun, and try to win.

Being out of the game, and sitting on the sideline watching everybody else run around the gym, throwing balls at each other, felt like being a bump on a log waiting for a chance to get off. I know this rather well because I was one of those non-removable types of bumps.

Now, this was Steve's first time playing the game, and if you remember, Eddie took him out early.

Even the best of the best has his/her bad day, and today was one of those days for Eddie. One of his archrivals, Edgar Valliant, from Mr. Augment's class, was one of the elite final eight players left standing in the game. The green ball rolled his way after bouncing off Gabby's leg. I do not recall who threw the ball, so don't ask me.

Edgar quickly picked up the green ball and held it behind his back. Then, he looked left, right, and left again. There standing dead ahead was none other than Eddie himself. Edgar inched closer and closer to Eddie at a snail's pace, hiding behind the remaining six gladiators of Beaver Ball. Finally, there was an opening for a clean shot. Edgar took a pitcher's stance, palmed the ball in his right hand behind his back, and hurled it directly at his target. Two seconds later, a loud *KABOOM* echoed throughout the gymnasium from the ball hitting Eddie square center in the middle of his chest.

A loud, deaf-piercing cheer full of screams and hollers emerged from the ten contestants of the game that were taken out earlier by Eddie. Quickly, each one of the ten players, except for me, hopped up from the sideline and reentered the game in hopes of being victorious.

I was one of the ten players taken out of the game by Eddie, but I decided to stay on the sideline watching. Before reentering the game, I looked over at Steve and saw a look in his eyes that gave me the chills. Therefore, I decided to sit back down to see what would unfold. Gabby and I sat together. She would help with some of the play-by-plays. Since I am telling you this story, I will do the editing and tell you what I think is necessary for you to know.

Steve now had his second chance at the game. He ducked, dodged, wiggled, and hopped over every ball that whizzed by him. He actually landed several good shots. But, before he knew it, little Liona Odessa from Mr. Augment's class picked up the yellow ball that rolled by her feet, walked over and stopped two feet from Steve. Next, she firmly pulled the ball toward her chest and pushed it like shooting a basketball with two hands, landing squarely on Steve's back.

Steve fell to the gym floor in agony while grasping his head with both hands. He cried, "No! No! No! No! It can't be! I got knocked out by Liona Odessa!"

Quickly, the seven students Steve knocked out of the game reentered, scattering like squirrels in the middle of a street with speeding cars.

Everybody left Liona alone since she was the most recent student to send Steve to the sideline. This was true until there were only three students left. You see, somewhere in all of the commotion, a ball luckily hit Edgar's leg. As he exited the game, Eddie returned and went on a rampage. But, as quickly as Edgar sat down, the student who hit his leg with a ball was hit with the red ball by Eddie. It was obvious to me that Eddie wanted to be one of the final three players left in the game. When Eddie reentered the game, he was on the prowl to take Edgar out in any way possible.

As Edgar snuck up behind Liona, Eddie clenched the blue bouncy ball so tight I thought I saw some air escape. Before Eddie could launch the ball at Edgar, Liona's girl intuition kicked in as Edgar approached her. Liona jumped vertically two feet into the air to miss Edgar's attempted throw at her feet. Next, she twirled around in midair while hurling the yellow ball she secretly had, nailing Edgar square in his chest. Like Steve, Edgar was in disbelief that he got taken out of the game by a girl, especially by Liona Odessa.

This act made Eddie boil over. He felt it was his duty to eliminate the person who had taken him out of the game. I believe this made him even more focused on taking Liona out of the game, just so he could have his chance at Edgar. That was how it came down to Liona and Eddie, a boy and a girl, being the last two players.

Eddie had a couple of choices. First, he could have been a good sport and had a tie game with Liona. Second, he could have allowed Liona, the only girl who had taken Steve and Edgar out of the game, to throw one of the balls and knock him out of the game, therefore prolonging it. The second choice would therefore, allow *ALL* of the other students except for Steve and Edgar to rejoin the game. However, at the time, that choice was not at the top of the Eddie's list.

It was like a gun fight from the old west. Eddie picked up the yellow and green balls, one in each hand, and Liona picked up the red ball. Eddie took his stance, stared down Liona, and yelled, "You're going down, Liona!"

She stood firmly in her place and just smiled. Eddie heaved the yellow ball as fast as he could, but Liona's quick reflexes blocked it with the ball she held firmly in her hands. The red ball did not budge an inch.

A wide-open gawk of surprise fell upon Eddie's face as he hollered in a squeaky voice, "I bet you can't do that again!" If my camera had been available, it would have made a perfect picture.

Again, Liona stood in place, not saying a word. She quietly smiled.

For his final chance, Eddie bounced the green ball a couple times while staring Liona down, just as a basketball player does when standing at the foul line attempting to make a free throw. Next, he firmly grasped the ball in his right hand after the final bounce, took a running stance, and shot off from his position like a runner racing at the Olympics. Upon his release point, the midcourt line of the gym, he threw the ball just as an outfielder does attempting to get a runner out at home plate. I mean, he really threw that ball fast.

Still in her same spot, Liona took a side step to her left to avoid being hit by the VFFB (Very Fast Flying Ball) as it flew by her, making her hair flutter as if she was outside at recess and a light wind had breezed by.

It seemed as if Eddie was in fifth gear as he continued running, making the sound of a car changing gears, even after he released the ball. Liona took half a step to the side and tapped him on his shoulder as he flew by. Eddie was so upset that he hit the pads on the wall under the basketball goal at full speed. He was okay, so there was no need to worry.

Seconds later, no players, except for Edgar and Steve, the two taken out of the game by Liona, sat furiously on the sideline. Slowly but surely, Eddie joined them. Gabby and I sat quietly on the sideline as the only two players who decided not to reenter the game.

In all the mayhem of students coming in and leaving the game, some lucky student, I could not see who, hit Liona on her left foot.

Poor Edgar! When he joined the game for the second time, he could no longer focus his eyes on Liona, the lucky girl who took him out of the game. Since she was out of the game, he had to focus elsewhere.

I understood how he felt, but sometimes that happened in this game. I continued to stay with Gabby because neither she nor I wanted to face the wrath of Steve, which would be unleashed along with Edgar's rush of fury.

Looking over at him just as Liona was hit on the leg by some lucky student, I could clearly tell Edgar's anger was about to boil over.

There were now only 12 minutes left on the wall clock. I asked myself, "Who will win? Can Steve do it? Only time will tell."

My hypothesis about Steve was validated when he went on a rampage, focusing on all of the weak players first. One by one each of the weaker boys and girls were knocked out of the game with ease.

Next, Steve focused on the players knocked out earlier who were about to rejoin the game for the second or third time. As soon as a player stepped back in the game, Steve would make a legal hit to end his or her chances for a victory.

While Steve was on his rampage, he kept a keen eye on his surroundings. I'll bet he was thinking, "I will not be hit in the back again by anyone, especially a girl!"

With each person that Steve took out of the game, he would laugh, "Now we will see who the best is!"

Sitting alongside of Gabby watching this massacre, I continued to keep a sharp watch on the wall clock. I wanted to see how long it would take Steve to win. The last gladiator standing in Steve's way was none other than Eddie Edge, the first player to take Steve out of the game.

Liona kept a sharp eye on the student who knocked her out of the game. The moment she stepped into the arena, Steve hit her on the foot with the red ball. I think Steve wanted to ensure his safety; he did not want to be hit in the back, especially by a girl!

I do remember Eddie reentering the game leaving Steve alone to his business and focusing solely on Edgar. Eddie ducked, dodged, hoped, and skipped over and under each ball that came his way. He did not even have enough time to pick up a ball. Luckily, Steve did most of the work for him. To make matters worse, one of the balls Steve threw hit Edgar in his right leg. Eddie was furious.

Gabby whispered, "Showdown between Steve 'The Bee' and Eddie 'Shouting' Edge." as I glanced at the clock to find that we only had five minutes left before declaring an ultimate champion.

Steve hoarded all three balls. With the green ball in hand, yellow ball between his knees, and the red ball firmly planted beside his feet, Steve took a crouching position. Steve stared Eddie down with the meanest look. It was one just like a mother would give her son or daughter if one did something on the most terrible, horrific level.

The question on all our minds, and probably Eddie's mind too was "What will Steve do next?"

Coach called out, "Three minutes left!"

Steve acted first. He yelled, "Thanks, Coach!"

Just as Eddie took his eye off of Steve to reply to Coach, Steve saw his opportunity for a shot. First, he quickly picked up the red ball from its still position with his left hand. Steve now had a ball in each hand. He then firmly drew back both balls behind his shoulders. At last, upon reaching the release point, Steve threw both balls in a most dramatic form.

Just as Eddie turned back to face Steve, the green ball hit both feet at the same time, and the red ball hit him squarely in the chest. Now, *that* is a two-for-one shot!

Both classes could not believe our eyes. Eddie Edge, one of the best at the game, had just lost to a rookie at the game of Beaver Ball.

Being a classy guy, a *REAL* sportsperson showing true sportsmanship, Eddie brushed off his shirt and immediately walked over to shake hands and congratulate Steve on his victory.

If you can recall the earlier situations Steve had been in, his consistency in showing good sportsmanship was remembered by neither students nor teachers.

Just under two minutes were left in class when Coach Tough announced on his personal microphone, "Congratulations, Steve! Class, let's show Steve what happens when we have an *ultimate* winner of Beaver Ball!"

Oh, I left out one important final rule of Beaver Ball because we very seldom, probably only once a year, if that, have an ULTIMATE winner of Beaver Ball. The final rule states:

When there is an *ultimate* winner of Beaver Ball, that student will stand in the middle of the game arena. Every player will then be given a ball by the supervisor of the game, Coach T. Those players then have the opportunity to throw their ball at the *ultimate* winner.

Coach quoted the rule to Steve, but Steve did not look too happy. I mean, how would you feel after just winning a difficult game, and then have to stand still while all the people you just knocked out of the game have a chance to throw a ball back at you?

As the last syllable came out of Coach T.'s mouth, Steve bolted for the gym doors, hit the arm bar at top speed, and continued out into the hallway with both hands flailing about yelling, "There is *NO* way I'm getting hit by anymore balls, especially one thrown by a *girl!*"

Coach T. quickly walked after him. A few of us tried to follow, but Coach turned around and boldly commanded, "Stay where you are. I don't want to see anyone leave this gym!"

At first, we did exactly what he ordered us to do. Just seconds later, what seemed like an eternity to most of us, curiosity took a huge bite of our juicy brains, getting the better of the majority of both classes, leaving all but a few students, Gabby, Liona, and me calmly sitting on the floor. The others skedaddled from their previously frozen spot, randomly arriving at the doors to peer out the windows into the hallway to see what was happening. The short students had to hop up and down like pogo sticks just to see over the shoulders of those standing in front.

Lo and behold, while Steve was running with his arms flailing and his head shaking, he smashed right into Triple P. I am pretty sure that Triple P. would have said something in his raspy voice like, "Why, hello there, Mr. Sting. What's the rush?"

Steve gasped for breath bending over his knees and lost his train of thought as he gazed into the gigantic eyes of Triple P.

Later on that day, I reviewed the day's video and was able to lip read. I noted that P. to the Third Power said something like, "Okay, Mr. Sting, why are you running in the hallway?"

Without speaking a word, Steve pointed toward the gym just as Coach T. came out of the gym calling, "Steve, stop running. Come back to class."

Coach T. and Triple P. guided Steve back to the gym. As soon as they turned the corner, all of those who peered out the windows rapidly scattered to their previous spots where they had been when Coach told us to stay put.

Again, neither Gabby, Liona, nor I got up from our spots because we did not want to get into trouble. We hoped that Steve would stand in the middle of the gym with assistance from Coach Tough and Triple P. We wanted him to be a good sport and take the hits by all of the players of the game.

Of course, that thought was only a dream because Steve did not look very happy when he reentered the gym with Coach T. and Triple P.

Triple P. patiently waited in the corner. Coach kneeled down, looked Steve straight in the eyes, and calmly said, "You played a magnificent game! We seldom have any *ultimate* winners of Beaver Ball. It would mean a lot to Triple P., your classmates, and me, if you would put on a brave face and stand in the middle of the gym to allow every player of the game the opportunity to throw the ball back at you."

For a second there, it looked as if Steve was about to turn over a new leaf and be a good sport by following the last rule of the game, and most of all, Coach T.'s polite request. But shortly, that idea vanished from my thoughts like roaches do from a bright light turned on in a dark room.

I'll give Steve credit. He was being polite by listening patiently, even though I could see he was still a little frustrated.

In addition to his request, Coach T. gave Steve three options:

1. Follow the rules of Beaver Ball.
2. Go see the school counselor to talk about whatever you want to talk about.
3. Lose recess and do the writing consequences for your actions today.

Steve caressed his chin thinking for a few seconds. He boldly declared, "I have decided to serve the writing consequence."

Triple P. motioned Steve to look at him and stated, "Steve you do know that if you make this choice, you will now have 50 sentences to write during recess. That means you will write 25 sentences on Wednesday and 25 sentences on Thursday."

Immediately, Steve graciously made his choice. He calmly agreed, "Okay, okay, I accept the writing consequence. I don't need to see the school counselor, and I refuse to stand in the middle of the gym and get hit by balls."

Coach T. held out his hand to seal the deal, and immediately Steve grasped ahold of it to agree with Coach and Triple P.

Both classes were so focused on watching Steve, wondering how he would shake hands with Coach T., we did not realize that Triple P. was no longer in the gym.

At that time, I thought, *Is Steve just kidding around, or is he serious?*

A minute later, both teachers, Mr. Prosper and Mr. Augment, entered the gym to pick us up. Directions were given to double step it to class because we were behind schedule. We had to get ready for the end-of-day procedures.

If you are keeping track, this is the second appearance of Triple P. (a.k.a. P. to the Third Power, or Pick on People Punisher). In a way, I would say that he has been a lucky charm both for Steve and for my class. Instead of breaking our current streak, Triple P. has been able to redirect Steve in a way that helps him rethink his actions so that he understands consequences.

While the announcements were blasting over the intercom, Mr. Prosper was kind enough to add one more positive day to the daily chart of the current streak. That made the end of the school day even better for us!

Day 1	Food Fight
Day 2	Start of New Streak (Day 1) YES
Day 3	Continuing Streak (Day 2) YES
Day 4	Continuing Streak (Day 3) YES
Day 5	Continuing Streak (Day 4) YES
Day 6	Continuing Streak (Day 5) YES
Day 7	Continuing Streak (Day 6) YES
Day 8	
Day 9	
Day 10	

Chapter 14
Just Three Days Left

Day 8

IT WAS NOW Wednesday, the middle of the week. Many of us couldn't wait for the weekend to arrive. Why do you ask? First, Friday was the last school day of the week. Second, that Friday marked an end to Mr. Prosper's substituting job; Mrs. Fair would be back the following Monday. Third, it was Halloween!

After going trick-or-treating, I, along with some of my good friends, planned to have a sleepover at my place. We would stay up late, talk about how much fun we had, and eat as much candy as we could, or as much as my mother would allow. Sadly, we all had to wait for that day to come. It was getting harder and harder for some of us to hold it together. Nobody in my class wanted to be the person to break the streak of setting a new school record. Oh, by the way, both records happened to be the same.

Day 7 was another day of all days to remember. There was an ultimate winner at Beaver Ball and Steve showed a little bit more respect and sportsmanship. It was a day that would stay in my elementary mind for a long time. Personally, I thought Steve's rampage was a little over the top. He was probably making up for the tetherball game he had lost to Pete, and the race he had lost to Daisy.

I hardly slept a wink that Tuesday night. All I could think about was how focused Steve had been on winning the game.

Well, there I was, first in class again sitting in my seat quietly, deep in my thoughts, not paying much attention to my classmates as they entered the classroom.

The hours seemed to just fly by. The only thing of importance worthy of telling you about is how Steve accepted his consequence. He kept the promise he had made to Coach T. and Triple P. Steve was a man (boy) of his word.

If Steve had not kept his word, he probably would have been sent to Principal Paige's office, therefore breaking the class/school's current streak, and nobody would trust him again, or want to play games with him, whether inside or outside at recess. He would forever be known as a *poor sportsman*, and a *sore loser*.

Mr. Prosper, with his many years of experience under his belt, recognized this. Since it was not in Mrs. Fair's lesson plan, he decided to make a change. Instead of being as intense as they normally were, they were a little more relaxed. I strongly believe that this change in plans made the day flow as easily as it did. I don't want to imagine what kind of day it would have been if Mr. P. had done everything as if it were a normal day.

Steve's behavior was top notch all day, even during ELT (usually Extended Laughing Time for him). No thought of a food fight crossed his mind during lunch, and social studies class was a breeze.

Before lining up to go out to recess, he asked, "Mr. Prosper, may I have a clipboard so I can do my writing consequence of 25 times?"

"Here you go, Mr. Sting," replied Mr. P. as he handed Steve his clipboard.

Immediately upon exiting the doors out to the recess area, Steve sat down against the wall by the door and began writing. I did not even see him look up one time during the entire recess. Judging the length of the sentence, I would guess that it would take the entire recess to write the sentence 25 times.

My friends and I were extremely proud of Steve for doing the right thing. He accepted his consequence without any signs of argument. Personally, I believe he was taking a breather from everything. But, who knows, perhaps this breather was all Steve needed to rejuvenate his mind and to recognize that all students, teachers, and staff here at Workaholic

Elementary really do care about one another, even when experiencing a *bad day*. With this thought in mind, a couple friends and I stood off in the distance watching and admiring how Steve took ownership of his consequences.

While we lined up for specials, P.E. again, a poem came to mind, which I had written last year. The names have been changed to protect the innocent.

"CLASS"

On a zero, no sound to be heard
Announced Billy May, the classroom nerd

Reading and writing is what we can do
There'll be no whining from you know who

Then one minute out of the blue
Heard whimpers come from Carrie Sue

Her very best friend for all her life
Said, "Buck up girl, here's a wipe!

Dry your tears and look at me
Class is over, it's time for P.E."

A few of us wondered what was on Steve's mind since this was his second time being in P.E. I was amazed at how calm he looked while standing in line next to the wall in front of Coach T. Instead of playing another game of Beaver Ball, Coach Tough decided to have us play a round or two of Round Robin. We played each game of basketball, beanbag toss, hula hoop, Frisbee toss, and Four Square for a few minutes before rotating. You know how it works.

The day ended with a smooth transition to the class and reflection time. Oh yeah, the table was filled in, too.

Day 1	Food Fight
Day 2	Start of New Streak (Day 1) YES
Day 3	Continuing Streak (Day 2) YES
Day 4	Continuing Streak (Day 3) YES
Day 5	Continuing Streak (Day 4) YES
Day 6	Continuing Streak (Day 5) YES
Day 7	Continuing Streak (Day 6) YES
Day 8	Continuing Streak (Day 7) YES
Day 9	Continuing Steak (Day 8)?
Day 10	

Chapter 15
The Day Before

Day 9

ALL REMAINED CALM in the fifth grade hallway. Even the *dragon*, Steve "The Bee" Sting, was at rest. I referred to him as a *dragon* here because when he was in his prank mood he could be like a scaly-flying beast releasing its fury by spitting fire and burning everything within its reach, and in this case, destroying the new streak we had going for setting the school record, which would leave nothing but dust from the hopes and dreams of students and teachers.

For all that he knew, the only person capable of putting out his fire was Principal Paige. With this in mind, Steve kept his pranking ways at bay. On Day nine of Mr. Prosper's assignment, there was no fooling around. Steve neither made a single sarcastic remark about anybody or anything, nor made any attempt to engage in competition in any way, shape, or form. Nothing that Steve did on Thursday stuck out to indicate he may be up to something in the near future, Friday perhaps.

I would make a wager that Steve's self-awareness was becoming better and better each day here at Workaholic Elementary. Steve knew, and so did everybody else, he hated to lose at anything he did and how he reacted inappropriately when and if he did lose.

When it was time for recess, Steve did exactly the same as on Wednesday; he asked Mr. Prosper for a clipboard and without hesitation began his writing consequence. Steve promptly handed in his work at the conclusion of recess. It was a nice breezy day, so I stayed in the shade and engaged in *people watching*.

Mr. Prosper pleasantly commended, "Very well done, Mr. Sting. I am proud of you for completing your consequence."

In response, Steve replied in a reassuring voice, "Thank you very much, Mr. Prosper."

Both teacher and student concluded with a firm handshake.

I think that I saw a few students watching off in the distance wiping their eyes. Were they crying in a happy way? Another thought crossed my mind. Did I *actually* see a gleam in Steve's eyes after he received the wonderful complement from Mr. Prosper?

A few seconds later, he rubbed his eyes with the sleeves of his shirt. Could it have been a tear from a shot of happiness from his heart peering out through his eyes, or was it from some dust flying around from the light breeze that day? Truly, I don't know, but knowing Steve, at least right then, the tears were probably from eye irritation from the dust, not from a shot of happiness.

Nothing ever worth talking about takes place during social studies class. The only thing I remember being spoken about was "Learn about the past so you won't repeat its failures," or something like that.

It was off to music class again, and most of us could not contain our emotions. Steve just stood in line emotionless. Judging from last week, his first time in music class, he did not want to let anyone know, at least at this time, that he really did enjoy singing. Instead of banging on drums and playing instruments, Mr. Chord continued working with us on our songs for the third annual Workaholic Elementary School Holiday Recital. Now, if you recall, Steve had a fabulous instrument, that meant, he sang effortlessly on key, much better than any of his classmates. Still, Mr. Chord had not approached Steve in front of his classmates.

Immediately upon arrival to Mrs. Fair's room from music class, Mr. Prosper filled in the chart for Day nine, and the class let out a light cheer. We did not want to have any fifth grade teachers come running over to our class again for loud noise, even at the end of the day.

Day 1	Food Fight
Day 2	Start of New Streak (Day 1) YES
Day 3	Continuing Streak (Day 2) YES
Day 4	Continuing Streak (Day 3) YES
Day 5	Continuing Streak (Day 4) YES
Day 6	Continuing Streak (Day 5) YES
Day 7	Continuing Streak (Day 6) YES
Day 8	Continuing Streak (Day 7) YES
Day 9	Continuing Streak (Day 8) YES
Day 10	

If my recollection was correct, I saw Mr. Chord speak to Mr. Prosper after school. Not that I was eavesdropping or anything, but I do remember the conversation's topic was about Steve's voice. Sitting just outside the room in the hallway at one of the kidney-shaped tables, I heard a high pitched voice screaming in excitement. There was no doubt it was Steve's mother because I have not heard of him talking about having any sisters, either older or younger. Who knows how she let Steve know of the news.

Before my mother called for me from the main hall, the thought, *hopefully* Steve took the news well, and *will continue* being his new self tomorrow, crossed my mind.

Chapter 16
Last Day of Assignment

Day 10

GUESS WHAT DAY it was? You got it. It was Halloween! It also marked the final day of the tenth day in a row that Mr. Prosper had substituted in my class. Now, I am not saying he never substituted for Mrs. Fair, another fifth grade teacher, or even another teacher again this year, just that it was the last day for his 10-day assignment. The other times Mr. Prosper substituted here at Workaholic Elementary School are another story.

Friday, October 31st, was one of a few special days we had. It was a school-wide event called the Fall Festival. A modified schedule was used; we did not have specials. Three question marks were inserted on Day 10 of Mr. Prosper's assignment, which was the same as Day nine of the school record. My thought was that Mr. P. placed them there as an incentive to keep the streak going, which neither student nor teacher wanted broken.

Day 1	Food Fight
Day 2	Start of New Streak (Day 1) YES
Day 3	Continuing Streak (Day 2) YES
Day 4	Continuing Streak (Day 3) YES
Day 5	Continuing Streak (Day 4) YES
Day 6	Continuing Streak (Day 5) YES
Day 7	Continuing Streak (Day 6) YES
Day 8	Continuing Streak (Day 7) YES
Day 9	Continuing Streak (Day 8) YES
Day 10	Continuing Streak (Day 9)???

I am going to warn you ahead of time. I decided to break this day down by the class period time because of the importance of the day. To some of you it may seem like a diary, but it's *NOT*. Boys my age do *not* have diaries. Call it an *agenda* of the day's events!

Of course I arrived at school early, just as I do every day, but today I arrived even earlier than usual. I sat patiently on the office couch with my backpack on one side and an old shopping bag with my costume in it on the other while my mother got her class ready for the two-hour school-wide Fall Festival.

Start	End	Class
	Mrs. Fair's Fifth Grade Modified Class Schedule	
7:20	8:00	Morning Work and Class Meeting
8:00	8:25	Reading
8:30	8:55	Math
9:00	9:25	Preparation for School Wide Event
9:30	11:30	School Wide Event (Fall Festival)
11:35	12:05	Lunch (Paid food brought to each grade level Teacher Workroom. Other bag lunches from cafeteria)
12:10	12:35	Recess
12:40	1:05	Language Arts
1:10	1:35	Social Studies
1:40	2:05	Science
2:10	2:25	Pack up, Reflection, review HW
2:30		dismissal

We received the flyer about the event a few weeks ago. It was in our Thursday folder. It was so important to us that our parents signed it that night, and it was returned on Friday. One-hundred percent of the flyers were turned in!

I guess that Steve's mother was given the flyer along with some other paperwork when he transferred here, probably before his first day, or some other point in time. The exact time does not matter, because he dressed up for the event anyway.

Even though the festivities took place on Halloween day, the administration, teachers, staff, and parents wanted us to use our hopes, dreams, and imaginations in a positive way. So, instead of calling it a Halloween party, we called it a Fall Festival. This was not the first time that the festival was planned this way. It's just that, being a child, we sometimes tend to forget the exact details of what happened during something like this one or more years ago.

Costume Guidelines

1. Costumes are to be homemade (no store bought costumes)
2. Scary (ghost, ghouls, goblins, witches, vampires, dead, etc.) are also prohibited
3. Costumes can be:
   a. What the student wants to be when he/she grows up
   b. A character from a book (excluding rule 2)
   c. A creation of the student's imagination (excluding rule 2)

The festival was described on the flyer, so I don't need to go into full detail. Like any flyer requiring parental permission, a box with "Yes" or "No" to check and a signature line was located at the bottom of the flyer. Oh yeah, there was also a charge of three dollars to cover the cost of food (pizza, drinks, chips, and fruit). If a student did not bring money, he or she would have to eat lunch from the cafeteria. I'll bet you want to know what every grade dressed up as, don't you? I will start with fifth grade.

Mrs. Fair's Class

Apple dressed up as Professor Adams, the most intelligent female scientist. She wore thick black glasses, a long white lab coat, pocket protector covered with pens, and some other scientific stuff.

Beverly wanted to be a journalist when she grew up. She wore a nice suit with the words "Ask Beverly" hand-embroidered across it, had a large red pen with sparkly-fluffy feathers in one hand, and in the other held a huge pink and white book to write all of her complaints in.

As professional as he could be, Cal dressed up as a businessman. His attire included a black suit with thin white vertical pinstripes, black shoes, black socks, and an earpiece for a cell phone in one ear; he held the cell phone in his right hand becoming a spitting image of his father.

Daisy had the most outrageous costume of all. Both her shirt and pants were some sort of black and white wavy lines. If any student stared at it too long, they would be put in a hypnotic trance and would be under her control.

Eddie decided he wanted to be a family doctor. He wore a long, white doctor's coat with a real stethoscope hanging around his neck. Some gizmo that doctors use to look in a patient's ear and a knee knocker were in his front left pocket.

Faith had on a matching shirt and pants set with book prints. On top of those prints were pictures of books of various shapes and sizes attached with Velcro.

A human-sized pen with a five-color top hat was the costume for Gabby. With both hands she carried a humongous book. The entire class made an educated guess that Gabby wanted to be a gossip columnist. If not that, some type of writer.

Hailey built a microphone from cardboard and a Styrofoam ball; decorating was spot on to a real microphone. She also had on an ear set headphone and a red shirt designed with "FM 88 WES" in huge black letters on the back and in small print on the top left corner on the front side. I guess that meant radio station 88 Workaholic Elementary School.

"Mr. Problem Solver" himself, Ian, being the great mediator he is, wore a collared shirt monogrammed with his saying "Come See Ian!" Every student in fifth grade knew his indisputable reputation for solving problems between students. He once told me, "My favorite subject is social studies." He also summarized some quote about the past and made it more his. He said, "Learning from the past helps to make a brighter future."

Julie wore one of the oddest costumes I have ever seen. Since she enjoyed arriving early to class on a daily basis, the theme of her costume was a clock. A mini grandfather clock, the size of an oversized piece of jewelry laid laced around her neck. On either side of it, the outline of an analogue clock laid in place, connected with a gold plated chain. Her pants were labeled "In Time" on her left leg and "Moves On" on her right. There was also some sort of bell inside her shoes, for each time she walked, the sound "Ting-tang" was emitted.

We all remember Steve gloating during morning meeting about how good of a football player he claimed to be. For this reason, he wore his football uniform, jersey, pads, and helmet; everything but cleats. He followed Principal Paige's rule of no cleats inside the school.

Tommy, with his high level of intelligence, decided to have fun, too. He had won some type of competition several months ago. The prize was a college scholarship. For this, his father gave him an undisclosed amount of money; he had never told me the exact amount, and I never asked. Somehow he got the brilliant idea to get a picture of a one-hundred dollar bill printed from the top of a shirt to the bottom of his pants. The front of him was the front of the bill, and his back was the back side of the bill. The costume represented that he planned to make a lot of money.

I, Gregory, dressed up as a cameraman. First, I made a camera out of cardboard. Second, I colored and decorated it. Third, I added wires with rolled up black construction paper and electrical tape. I strapped my real camera around my neck and body. It was in front of me while my fake camera lay on my back, pointing behind me. My silkscreened shirt had "GTV" on the front and "Cameraman" on the back.

One thing Principal Paige did not allow was for students to wear cleats because neither she nor Mr. Hardly, the school head custodian, (who never missed a day of school) wanted the floors to get scratched or scuffed up.

Mrs. Easel's Class

Kevin dressed as a professional kickball player. He wore matching red, white, and blue wrist and headbands, a red number "1" jersey with his name "KEV" on the back in white, and a blue pair of shorts. He also had on a brand-spanking new pair of Nimblers, even newer than Steve's.

Leslie somehow dressed up exactly as Valerie. One could almost say they were twins, but that did not sit too well with Valerie because she believed as she had gloated many times before, "*I am the one and only beauty queen of fifth grade!*" If I recall correctly, their mothers knew each other and were best friends since grade school, and Valerie's mother may have spilled the beans on what Valerie was going to wear.

It was no girly costume for Melony. An automobile mechanic was her choice. Having two older brothers, one in middle school, one in high school, and a father who owned an auto repair shop, Melony was constantly around cars. Every day after school the bus dropped her off at the shop. I bet she watched her father every day and would help him at home sometimes, too.

Nancy's mother made one of the most colorful and highly imaginative costumes I have ever seen. It was a green bookworm with red, orange, yellow, and blue designs all over it. The costume even had kinks to bend and sway just like a worm moves, except she was standing, not wiggling on the ground. Of course, she wore a giant pair of glasses, too. I believe it was one of the top three costumes of the whole school.

Oscar loved to play soccer, and for the festival he dressed as his favorite professional soccer player, Johnny "Swift" Jackson. Oscar looked like the player in every way possible, even the hair. No cleats for Oscar, either.

The reigning champion of tetherball, Pete, dressed as a surfer. I noticed his great balance during his match, so I could visualize him on a surfboard in the ocean waves. Pete changed into swim trunks and water shoes, and carried a well-painted surfboard, probably made out of a few pieces of Styrofoam joined together with large and pointy wooden skewers. It was beautiful!

When it was time do dress out, Quade gently removed his long, white lab coat with different math signs (multiply, divide, add, and subtract), and answers to equations with no show of work from his rather large gift bag, which must have been from his last birthday. He pushed up his glasses, stepped up on his chair, and boldly announced, "I am Q Squared, the quickest and smartest mathematician in fifth grade!"

Randy, the nature guy, brought a rather large brown bag to hide his brown bear costume. It looked exactly like a brown bear, with fur, teeth, eyes and all. Some time that day, he told me he had been working on the project since the first day of class.

Urquhart's costume was a different story, totally different from the rest of the class. He created a magnificent replica of the Loch Ness Monster from Scotland. I told you earlier that he spoke with an accent; well, it's Scottish.

Valerie, the beauty queen, wore a dazzling dress that looked exactly like the one some little princess wore in a movie she constantly talked about. Valerie's mother was a miracle worker with a sewing machine. It must have taken her at least a week to complete the dress, working on it when she got home from her job at the beauty salon as a hair stylist.

When the time arrived, Wayne appeared in the hall as a coach. His favorite teacher was Coach T. Wayne had at least three whistles around his neck, wore a hat with "COACH" on it, and also had on a track jump suit. He looked like a real coach. I believed being a coach was a wonderful career.

Xavier, the tough guy, entered the hallway as a pro boxer with "Double X" embroidered across his fire brick red shirt. A matching long silk robe with white borders, sky-blue towel draped around his neck, a pair of red, white, and blue calf-high socks, and black boxing shoes completed his costume. A friend assisted with putting on the gloves, personally made from smooth, thick cloth, filled with soft stuffing. The stitching was his. For a tough guy, he sure could stich.

Yancey, The Clumsy, as his classmates called him, wore red tights with a black "A" stitched in the middle surrounded by a blue and green boarder. Calf-high boots completed the costume. When asked who he was, he stated with a smile, "No longer will I be called Yancey, The Clumsy! I will now and forever be known as Yancey, The Agile!"

Zachary, or Zac, as his friends call him, decided that he needed no costume. Sitting on top of his high horse filled with an abundance of self-confidence, he only dressed in his brand new, steam-pressed orange-collared shirt and midnight-black khaki pants, a matching tie, black dress socks, and pointed toe, black dress shoes. I thought he should get off of his high horse and come down to Earth to join the rest of us fifth graders.

Mr. Augment's Class

Ever since first grade, Alice had been at the top of the class. She was an intelligent girl. All morning she had been in another room testing for advanced classes in middle school. She wore a black leotard with a bright shooting star across it. Various sized sparkles of stars and colors of space matter filled in, leaving just enough blank spaces.

Brian's move to southern California had left a big impact on him. He wanted to follow in his father's footsteps to be a jet pilot. While going to school in California, his father bought him a jet pilot outfit, which included a helmet, mask, dog tags, sunglasses, coveralls, and shoes. Brian was an exact replica of his father, even twin-like.

Just like Brian, Cedric dressed as a jet pilot. The outfit he wore was probably ordered from a magazine Brian let him borrow. In the hallway, Cedric announced, "My call sign is 'Hawk,' and Brian's call sign is 'Eagle'" as he showed all of us the two patches. Brian seemed confused yet happy at the same time as he gladly accepted the patch. I would wager that Brian would be the lead pilot and Cedric the Radar Intercept Officer (RIO) if they ever flew together.

Devin dressed up as a chef. She no longer wanted to be known just as a devourer of food, for her numerous food eating championships. From now on she wanted to be known as Chef Devin, a professional with immaculate taste buds and cooking credentials. Sometime that day she shyly whispered, "I am retiring my championship belt as a food eating competitor. Plan to see me in the cooking winner's circle soon!"

If you found an old dictionary in your parent's library, or searched on the World Wide Web for the word "gentleman," you would see a picture of Edgar, or at least his costume. Picture somebody in a nice, clean tuxedo-like suit, with a bow tie, shiny black shoes, and gold-plated cuff links. When he stepped out of the restroom all decked out, every single girl and female teacher stopped to take a look.

You can probably guess what Francis dressed as. Yep, you got it, a basketball player. One day during recess, before Steve transferred here, he showed me a couple of tricks, saying, "Just wait until our school festival! I will be a pro at it." His hypothesis was spot on. As the fifth grade walked around showing off our costumes, he magnificently performed for everybody.

A new hairstyle, clothes to match, a pen to sign autographs, and a real microphone were a dead giveaway for Gail's choice to be a singer. It was almost as if she was going to perform.

If you ever saw an artist from France in a movie, Hue was the artist. The beret, paintbrush behind his ear, and the canvas he carried with one of his best works made it realistic.

Girls at Workaholic Elementary chanted "You have been Isabeled" when something spectacular happened to them. Isabel's costume consisted of a sparkly dress she created, decorated handbag, and personalized shoes. She was the gossip of all the girls for the day.

Jennifer, the girl who knew just about everything about geography/social studies, dressed as an explorer. Her costume was as close to perfection as possible; it looked just like the pictures in the books we read. For an extra effect, she carried around an optical telescope.

A rather simple costume with the words, "I AM A WRITER" printed in deep-bold multi-colored letters was Kellie's choice of costume. Several books of various sizes and colors were attached to her shirt. She happily told me, "The names of the books are yet to come!"

Just imagine safety goggles in front of thin, light-red glasses, dirty blond hair sticking up from stress, a long white lab coat with spots of various colors and thicknesses, and a name tag stating Dr. Odessa, and you will see Liona. Yes, a doctor is her plan for the future. Talented that she is in all fields, she has plenty of time to make a final decision; yet, she is currently undecided.

My man, Marty, the so called *taker of bets no teacher knows about* knew his costume could not be a bookie Instead, he played it safe and dressed as a Four Square champion with gym shorts, ankle-high multi-colored socks, and wore brand new, high-grip Grapples. He even carried a red and black striped rubber ball. The moment he bounced it Principal Paige scolded, "Who dares bounce a ball on my shiny floor?"

Exact details of what the younger grades dressed as were not important to me. To be nice, after reviewing the tapes for fifth grade, I reviewed the other grades so I could give you a brief detail of their costumes. If I thought hard, I could see my friends and me as younger versions of us.

Fourth Grade

The theme for fourth grade was, "I want to be _____ when I grow up." Mrs. Trial's, Ms. Drudge's, and Mr. Sweat's students dressed in a pleasant mixture of careers, but not as much of a mixture as fifth grade. Mostly, there were doctors, lawyers, firemen, bakers, and teachers. Maybe next year when my classmates and I are gone, their costumes will be just as good as ours were.

Third Grade

Third graders used a little bit more imagination with their costumes than the fourth graders did. From what I heard, and briefly saw, each of them wrote a personal book. There was a variety of fiction, nonfiction, and even a few autobiographies. Mr. Struggle's, Ms. Grind's, and Mrs. Hailey's students decorated their own t-shirt with the words "I am _____." Each student also held their personalized book in one hand while walking down the hall.

Second Grade

Each second grade teacher, Ms. Scheme, Mr. Deed, and Mrs. Gaines (my mother), asked their students to pick his or her favorite animal book. This was perfect for a zoologist. I saw magnificent lions, tigers, bears, fish, penguins, whales, sharks, turtles, and a few other animals I did not recognize.

Now that I think of it, I do recall seeing my mother staying up late a few nights helping put together some of the costumes.

First Grade

Imagination was the theme for first grade. Mrs. Stint's, Mr. Grindstone's, and Ms. Toile's students were asked, "If you could be any-body you wanted to be, who would it be?" Oh, if you could see what I saw. These costumes were as creative as the fifth graders' costumes were. I saw a couple of presidents, some famous sports stars, actors, singers, dancers, firefighters, policemen, teachers, and even the students themselves.

Kindergarten

I remember long ago, only five years ago for me, what I did in Kindergarten. That year I dressed as my favorite animal, but this year each class chose their own theme. Students in Mr. Hobby's class read a book about some hero that was a fish. They all had on costumes of different colors made out of construction paper.

Mrs. Attempt's class read about farming. Each student had on a hat with colored cutouts of his/her favorite farm animal. A few mothers assisted in the decorating of the costumes.

Ms. Travail's class loved the bird books she had been reading, so they each picked a favorite bird and created very interesting costumes. If asked, I believe I could tell what most of them were. Somebody told me that a few of Ms. Travail's friends were able to help the class by gathering some real bird feathers.

Administration

Principal Paige dressed as a Supreme Court Judge. She wore a hand-sewn long, black robe that was a perfect replica of a real one, just like the one I saw on the news channel of some special report. She carried a gavel in one hand and the sound block, the thing a judge hit the gavel on, around her neck.

Assistant Principal Ericson, whom I have not mentioned because he usually handled matters dealing with Kindergarten through second grade, dressed as a fireman. From what I remember, he went to classes explaining the importance of following directions the first time and teaching the school song. Also, if any sort of behavior problem showed its face, he would be called to tame the flame before it had a chance to grow. Luckily, so far that year, he had yet to be called.

Our office secretary, Ms. Inquisitive, told me the morning of the Fall Festival, "If I was not working here at Workaholic Elementary School, I would write for the local newspaper and 'Ask Ms. Inquisitive' would be the title of my column." For that reason, her attire was business casual. Her suit was neither too businesslike nor too casual. I think it looked pretty keen and it fit her just right. Think about it, students sat in her area waiting before and after school telling her all sort of things, asking her for advice.

Chapter 17

Fall Festival

Day 10 continued

CLOSE YOUR EYES for a moment and use your imagination. I'll bet that you could picture yourself as one of the students, *maybe* even - dressed in costume for Workaholic Elementary School's fifth annual Fall Festival.

Silently, think to yourself, and if you are with a reading buddy, contemplate the same question, "What do I think Steve will do next?" Keep reading to find out, and whatever you do, please do not skip to the end of the chapter or the book, because you will miss the *GOOD* parts!

The modified schedule did not allow for much work to get done, and Mr. Prosper knew that before the day's lessons began. Instead of the usual workload, Mr. Prosper, with the okay of Mrs. Fair and the other fifth grade teachers, decided to mix up the day by having a review in a fun and competitive setting for each subject. It was boys versus girls. I would love to say that the boys demolished the girls every time, but it was the other way around a couple of times.

Mr. Prosper dug deep into his creative spirit and dressed as a game show host. He had on a black suit with white pinstripes with a white dress shirt, black shoes and dress socks, and a colorful tie with the words: THINK BEFORE YOU SPEAK. He was kind enough to bring his recently purchased, decked out, top of the line, Larynx 3000 karaoke machine, which had only been in the music store for a few days in limited supply. It had all the bells and whistles. Who would have thought that the best substitute ever, Mr. Prosper, would be one of the lucky three to own such a fabulous machine?

You may ask yourself, "How did such a quiet guy like Gregory Gaines know so much about a karaoke machine?"

The answer to said question is my cousin on my father's side of the family. Every July we have a family reunion. He was in a band in high school and hosts karaoke parties for a company he works for. He knows everything about old and new models before they come out in stores. A few weeks before the Fall Festival, he sent me a music magazine with the exact model Mr. Prosper bought. Sure wish you were here to see it!

Now for the rules of a regular game and a sudden death (tiebreaker) game:

Regular Rules: Boys versus Girls

1. A team captain from each side will draw a number from a hat to see who goes first.
2. Each team captain will nominate a scorekeeper for his/her team.
3. The game show host will select an official timekeeper.
4. A time of fifteen minutes will be set for each match (subject).
5. When it is their turn, each team has 21 seconds to answer the question.
6. If an answer is not given within the 21 seconds, or the answer given is incorrect, the other team has a chance to answer the question within 10 seconds.
7. All correct answers are worth one point in the form of a tic mark.
8. Zero (0) points are awarded for incorrect answers.
9. At the end of the match, points will be calculated.
10. If there is a tie score, the tiebreaker rules will go into effect.

Both boys and girls huddled on opposite sides of the room to decide on their captain and scorekeeper. Mr. Prosper decided who would have the title, *Official Timekeeper.*

Cal and Gabby were the captains, Daisy and Ian were the scorekeepers, and Faith was announced as the *Official Timekeeper.* Tiebreaker players, if needed, were decided by a unanimous vote at the end of the match.

The competition, albeit fun, became a little heated at one point. Mr. Prosper stepped in, and in his soft, calming, reassuring voice said, "Boys and girls, I can see you all are enjoying our friendly competition, but some of us are taking it a little too seriously. Remember, the only prize is your education, so do not get upset if you do not know the answer. Settle down and have fun."

Our so-called, *friendly competition,* as Mr. Prosper liked to call it, consisted of five matches (reading, math, language arts, social studies, and science), each named after the current subject.

Still in the spirit of his character as a game show host, Mr. Prosper gracefully picked up the microphone from atop the karaoke machine, turned both on, and called out: "Ladies and Germs! Whoops, I mean gentlemen. It is now time to begin the first of its kind, only here at Workaholic Elementary, a best of five matches! Here on my left, I have the Wild Boys, and on my right are the Sassy Girls."

Momentarily stunned from such an amazing skill just witnessed, Mr. Prosper added, "Scorekeepers and official timekeeper please take your places so we can begin."

Without hesitating, we all took our places. With valiance, we all gave Mr. Prosper *that look,* the one a student silently gives a teacher to verify readiness. Deep down each team strongly believed 101 percent they would be victorious.

Reading

Our competition started off with the Reading Match. It was quite a show of lesson comprehension since school started in August. Well before the 10 second allotted time for each team question, an answer was shouted out with glee by either the boys or girls, depending on whose turn it was.

The next thing we knew, "Time is up, time is up," squawked the parrot timer. Scorekeepers were instructed to calculate the total by circling tic marks into groups of five, and to put the total amount of points in a box.

Daisy quickly calculated her team's points and joyfully shouted at the top of her lungs, "Sassy Girls have 15 points!"

In his manliest voice, Ian yelled, "The Wild Boys have 15 points!"

You as well as I know that this meant that a tiebreaker round was next. After little deliberation, the Sassy Girls chose Beverly to represent them, and the Wild Boys chose Tommy.

Imagine if you will, Mr. Prosper standing in front of the room, decked out in his duds with Beverly standing in front of the desk on his right and Tommy standing in front of the desk to his left, each with a soft, squishy red and black accordion-like toy as a buzzer, which sat on top of three old, thick fifth grade math books. It squeaked like a duck when pressed. Quite a sight, if I do say so myself.

Sometimes there would be a tie score at the end of regular play. When that happened, a new set of rules came into play. We called it the *tiebreaker round*. This round was even more intense at times than the regular ones.

Tiebreaker Rules

1. Each team will choose one player.
2. The clock will be set for five minutes. Timekeeper will remain the same.
3. Scorekeepers will remain the same.
4. One point is given for each correct answer.
5. Correct answers equal a one (1) point gain.
6. Incorrect answers equal a one (1) point loss.
7. The player who presses his/her button first MUST answer within 10 seconds.
8. After either an incorrect answer or NO answer, the opponent has 10 seconds to:
   a. Answer the question for a one (1) point gain or loss, OR
   b. Say "Pass" to go onto the next question.

9. At the end of the five minutes, points will be tallied.

10. The team with the most points will be declared the winner of the match.

Cutting the details short, the match went back and forth with mostly correct and very few incorrect answers. Ultimately, we, the Wild Boys, were victorious with a score of 10 to 9. I was quite surprised we boys did not gloat too much. I mean, we did beat the girls at reading, and most every student has heard *girls are better readers than boys*, and this had just been proven wrong.

A quick two-minute break to catch our breath, bring us back down to Earth, and get a sip of water if needed was permitted before the second match in math began. A thirty-second countdown was given for all competitors to take his and her place to begin the scary, for some students, subject of math.

Math

Luckily, for a brief time, the boys were annihilating the girls in this match, one of Steve's favorite subjects. For some unknown reason, he was glued to his seat, furiously writing in his journal. Steve hardly paid any attention to the grueling match. You as well as I know how Steve extremely dislikes losing a competition, especially to a girl.

I whispered to myself, "*Why* was Steve so focused on writing in his journal instead of competing in the match against the girls?" I'm pretty sure nobody heard me. It's a good thing, too. They may have thought I was a little crazy.

For the Math Match, Mr. Prosper wrote an equation on the board and a player from each team raced to the board to solve it. Sometimes on a tough equation, a player waited in anticipation hoping their opponent wrote down the incorrect answer, so he/she would have a chance to steal the point by writing the correct answer.

With a quick glance at the clock, Mr. P. called out, "This is the last question," as he wrote it on the board. Tommy and Beverly quickly jumped out of their seats, rushed to the board and attempted to solve the equation.

Time was ticking away, second-by-second. Would there be a tie, sending us to a tiebreaker round? Or would we get a head start to get ready for the Fall Festival?

Mr. Prosper started the countdown at ten, and before he reached one Steve hollered out the answer and Tommy wrote it down. Beverly waited patiently to see if Steve was correct, tapping her fingers against her legs as beads of sweat poured down her face.

With a quick glance at the answer card, Mr. P. slowly looked up in dismay, and facing the boys' team, lifted the microphone to his lips and announced, "I am sorry, but that is incorrect."

Steve could not believe what he just heard. The entire class was shocked into disbelief.

Mr. Prosper quickly turned toward Beverly and in his game show host voice announced, "Sassy Girls, you now have a chance to steal a point. If you are correct, you will be the winners of the match. Do you have an answer to the equation?"

Beverly shyly turned to her team for help. They quickly huddled together. Narrowly escaping having a tiebreaker match, they shouted the answer with only one second left before the parrot timer squawked, "Time is up, arr! Time is up, arr!"

Imagine, if you can, every single boy (Wild Boys) on his knees trying to distract the girls by hollering out different numbers in an attempt to distract the Sassy Girls.

Beverly quickly wrote the answer on the board and then slowly placed the marker in the cup beside the board. She turned and faced Mr. P. in hope that her answer was correct.

The boys' chance of winning was about to be flushed down the drain. To no avail, all of the hooting and hollering was pointless.

Seconds later, Mr. Prosper took hold of the microphone, cleared his throat, flicked the switch on the karaoke machine to the *Open Mic* setting and in a tone neither I nor anyone else had heard before, he announced: "Boys and girls of Workaholic Elementary School, here in Mrs. Fair's class we have a winner! Sassy Girls have 18 points and the Wild Boys have 17 points. The Sassy Girls are the winners of the Math Match. Boys, good luck next April!"

Despite our amazement of Mr. Prosper along with our brief feeling of dismay, in a competitive spirit Steve hollered, "Hey girls, we want a rematch. This April, the Wild Boys **WILL** be victorious!"

Preparation for Fall Festival

It was time for the girls to get their heads out of the clouds and for us boys to get our minds straight for the Fall Festival. Even with Steve's last remark, the good sports people we were, we shook hands before being released to change into our costumes for the day.

Even being one of the first few boys in the restroom to change, Steve was still the last boy out, and the last to return to class. Maybe it just took him a long time to change, or perhaps he was up to something. I don't know. None of my classmates nor I noticed anything upsetting about his behavior. He was happy as a clam. At least that was what he portrayed himself to be on the outside. We had no idea if anything was boiling up on the inside, waiting for the right moment to erupt like an active volcano. Mentally, my senses were tuned in to Steve's frequency, but I was *NOT* about to allow what he was/was not going to do affect my fun time at the Fall Festival.

Fall Festival

Finally, after what seemed like forever, Steve exited the restroom. He was just in time for the fifth grade to line up for the event. My senses were still on high alert at Level five with Level seven the highest, just in case Steve thought about trying something mischievous to ruin the Fall Festival.

Imagination is a wonderful thing to have and to use as often as possible. So, dig deep and picture the costumes elegantly worn by each student walking down the main hallway, waving, smiling, and posing for pictures before returning to his/her designated hallway. Quite the site, if you imagine it that way. Of course, since I was a cameraman, I did take some memorable pictures for everybody to see. Some even made the yearbook.

I almost forgot an important part of the event, the music. Our trusty Hailey set the timer on the radio station to start playing fun, upbeat music she had created on her personal computer at home. It started approximately the same time the Kindergarten classes entered the main hallway.

Man, let me tell you, this music was groovy! A few students, and yes, teachers too, strolled out of line, moving and dancing to the intense beat. What a site! For a second, I thought I saw Mr. Prosper move a little to the fabulous tunes.

As the fun intensity increased to a level beyond comprehension, I lost track of Mr. P. He probably had something he had to do and asked another teacher to keep an eye on his class for a few minutes.

During all of the fun, I thought I saw Steve staring into a hallway window as we walked, probably to see his reflection. Suddenly, he vigorously shook his head like a person does when he or she sees something shocking. Steve even gave his face a couple slaps to wake himself up. But, when Steve looked in the reflection of the next window, he immediately turned around to look in all directions as if he was trying to locate a specific person in a crowd.

I was just a few classmates behind him and saw the whole thing. I asked myself, *what* in the world did Steve see? *Could* it be Triple P.? NO! *Perhaps* it was just his mind playing tricks on him. Whatever it was, Steve's demeanor changed for the good. The slight increase in my keen senses zeroed in on Steve and dropped from its current level to the lowest, Level one.

Well, before we knew it, the school-wide Fall Festival walk concluded and we were back in our classes. Hailey rushed to the audio/video room to change the tunes for a smooth and relaxing mood to help calm students as they transitioned to lunch.

Lunch

Some students had visions of devouring pre-paid pizza, chips, fruit and soda, while others had dismal pictures of slowly munching on a peanut butter and jelly sandwich on whole wheat bread squashed by a juicy red apple and sweet potato chips stuffed into a paper bag, along with bottled water, while watching classmates in agony, thinking, *why didn't I do what Mom and Dad told me to do so I could get the three dollars for pizza?* Happily, that was not the case for my class.

The upbeat tempo transitioned to a more calming, mellow vibe as each class entered their designated hallway, and somehow the pizza mysteriously arrived in each grade-level teacher's workroom. A couple of days prior to the school-wide event, Mrs. Inquisitive placed the rather large order. Each class received three pizzas with the topping they voted on, enough for each student to have two pieces. The sodas, water, and a variety of fruit were already in coolers and had been placed in the refrigerator before school started.

Most of us kept our costumes on to stay in the spirit of the festival, even Mr. Prosper. Before Eddie, Beverly, and Daisy could step one foot out the classroom door to pick up their cold, brown bag lunches, Mr. Prosper quickly took hold of the microphone, flipped the switch on the karaoke machine again, and ever so gently raised the microphone to his lips. "Stop in the name of pizza!" in a perfect tenor clef (just learned in music class) floated through the air on sound waves to our ears from Mr. Prosper's perfectly tuned vocal chords, tickling not only the hairs on our necks, but all over our bodies as well.

The three stopped dead in their tracks. I heard a few classmates whisper in surprised voices, "*Wow*! I did not know Mr. Prosper could sing so well!"

Hailey heard Mr. Prosper's voice as she was returning to class. Her eyes enlarged to more than three times the normal size when she entered the room, passing Eddie, Beverly, and Daisy. Covering half her mouth with her hand, Hailey turned around, faced us, and whispered, "Mr. P. has a wonderful singing voice and is quite the actor!"

With microphone in hand, Mr. Prosper motioned for the three to return to their seats, and while still in character sang, "Ladies and gentleman, please, oh, please come back to us. You don't need to eat that peanut butter and jelly. I know that you know you want pizza!"

Being the nicest man, substitute teacher that he is, Mr. Prosper pulled out the permission slips from the thick envelope on Mrs. Fair's desk, quickly shuffled through them, pulling out each slip of the student standing before him, showing each of them that the box marked PAID was checked.

Each one of them, in their own way, scratched his/her head in confusion with the prior knowledge that, in fact, the money had NOT been paid for some undisclosed reason(s). But, why the money was not paid earlier was of no importance to Mr. Prosper. They stood in front of Mr. P. dumfounded, shocked beyond belief muttering, "But. How? What?"

Mr. Prosper just smiled and whispered, "I reviewed all of the non-paid slips and paid the three dollars myself. I did not want any of my boys and girls missing out on the pizza with the rest of the class."

Now, tell me, *what substitute teacher* do you know of would have done, or even thought of doing, what Mr. Prosper did? *Slim* to *none*, right! The latter is more likely!

Without all the boring details, we devoured our two pieces of mouth-watering cheese pizza, quickly munched chip by chip, and guzzled our sodas and water, and finished the meal by sinking our teeth into reddish-green apples before heading out to recess.

Recess

The younger students in Kindergarten to second grade were too exhausted to change and go outside for recess. Instead, they had an indoor recess while third, fourth, and fifth graders went outside for an extended recess.

Hailey quietly tiptoed up behind Mr. Prosper and snatched the microphone from atop the karaoke machine while Ian turned it on. Briefly shocked, Mr. P. stood firmly grasping his chin with his left hand while crossing his chest with the other in anticipation of what was yet to come.

Seconds before the parrot alarm clock would squawk "Time for recess, time for recess!" Hailey dug deep for courage and sang, "Recess! Recess! It's here at last! We always have *FUN*! So, come on, let's go, and have a blast!"

Looking left, then right, Hailey added, "Last one out is a *rotten egg*!" before tossing the microphone back on top of the karaoke machine and racing outside.

For a split-second, we all glanced at each other, smiled, then simultaneously all jumped out of our chairs and shoved them up under our desks while Tommy hollered, "Let's hightail it out of here. I'll see you *rotten eggs* on the playground!"

Besides the extremely lousy disregard of the English language and what Hailey had been taught throughout her school career, the song was pretty cute. Mr. Prosper stood in one place in the middle of the room lost in nostalgia remembering the past when he was our age, frozen like a statue watching his (Mrs. Fair's) students break from the friendly competitive atmosphere he had created.

Steve was the last fifth grader outside to recess, but nobody dared to call him a *rotten egg*. For a brief second, the entire playground froze as Steve opened the side door and stepped foot on the playground. Everyone stopped and stared awaiting Steve's next move. Surprising to all, the magnificent true smile on his face showed neither a trace of ill thought nor a hint of sarcasm. Oddly, he seemed to be normal, with respect to Workaholic Elementary School standards.

Hold on! You don't think he did anything crazy do you? Well, he didn't. Calmly, he sat with his back against the reddish brick wall, smiled and watched everybody else have fun as he continued writing in his journal, but not so furiously this time. All of the yelling, screaming, running, and playing did not seem to bother him. Of course, we did not play rough enough to mess up our costumes. We still had three other matches, and we did not want to face the wrath of our parents by showing up at home with a ruined costume.

Language Arts

We had absolutely zero seconds to waste when we entered the classroom from recess. Of course, there was a brief restroom and water break before resuming Mr. Prosper's so called *friendly competition*.

Julie stood up in front of the class to lead us in a relaxation technique. In a calm, mellow voice she requested, "Stand up slowly by your desk. Close your eyes. Breathe in slowly through your nose. Hold it. Now, breathe out slowly through your mouth." The room became quiet and peaceful.

Suddenly, in an even softer voice, Mr. P. announced, "Boys and girls, take your places for the Language Arts Match."

After a stomach-filling lunch, a not so active recess, and a wonderful calming exercise, the Wild Boys could not focus. A few of us just about took a catnap. Some of the girls did not want both pieces of pizza, so each gave one piece to one boy. I believe the girls' sneaky plan of making the boys tired through overeating actually worked. During the exercise, with my eyes squinted just a tad, I bore witness to all of the Sassy Girls watching the

Wild Boys do the exercises. I continued so I would not give up what I knew.

Using what knowledge I had, I figured out that more than likely, the Wild Boys would not win this match. Instead of partaking in the Sassy Girls' slaughtering of us innocent victims, I sat quietly studying my notes from social studies, preparing for its match. The final score was a devastating, at least to the boys, score of 22 to 11.

To pour salt on the Wild Boys' wounds, one of those Sassy Girls wrote a nice little poem for us. It was left on my desk so I could read it to my team.

"RAIN"

Rat, tat, rat, tat, tat
Ting, tang, ting, tang, tong
Rata, tata, tat
Ting, tanga, tong

Rain, rain, rain
All day long

Bucket here, bucket there
Gotta put the buckets everywhere

Drip, drop, drip, drip, drop
Plop, fizz, plop, plop, fizz

Ringa, tanga, ting
Tinga, tanga, tong

Rain, rain, rain
All day long
RAIN

On the backside of this little poem was a note from the Sassy Girls. It read:

Hey Wild Boys! Pay attention to the fabulous words in this poem we wrote. This is what we are going to do to you in the next round. We are going to earn more points than you can count! Hope you guys *enjoyed* the pizza!

I could see fumes rising from some of heads of my teammates. Before becoming engulfed with madness, I knew I had to step up to the plate before the Social Studies Match began. I, Gregory, the "Quiet Student" actually spoke up to the boys. Usually I barely said a word, but when it came to winning, especially against a girl, I was in it 100 percent. I stood up tall on my chair, stared down below at my team, and shouted:

Snap out of it Wild Boys! Get a hold of yourselves! The Social Studies Match is next, and we have got to win! Ian, I know you are highly knowledgeable in the subject, and so am I. Let's win this match like it's the last one you will ever play!

My fellow Wild Boys and I huddled together to strategize our plan to be victorious in the next match. This time we meant business. We were not going to fall for any more sneaky tricks from the Sassy Girls!

Social Studies

It was now time for business. Ian and I knew we had the entire team behind us as we returned the favor to the Sassy Girls. We demolished them! I mean, they never knew what hit them. We answered every question asked within five seconds. The girls were so shocked, they lost track of what was going on and failed to answer the majority of the questions asked. I vaguely remember them only answering three questions correctly to our massive 29 points.

We took the win with dignity, although it took a lot for a few of my teammates to hold the gloating in because they knew there was one match left. The five minute break left enough time for both teams to shake hands and regroup before the final match. With the game tied at two matches each, the ultimate question on everyone's minds was *who will win the final challenge and have bragging rights until April's rematch, the Sassy Girls, or the Wild Boys?*

Science

The time on the classroom clock froze at 1:40 p.m. We all knew that meant it was time for the Science Match, the final battle. We, the Wild Boys, felt like we were floating on cloud nine after winning the Social Studies Match. Perhaps the Sassy Girls saw this as an opportunity to take before we could bring ourselves back down to Earth, or were we just playing possum?

Now back to reality! Let me tell you, this match was a fierce one. Point after point was earned, with very few incorrect and/or stolen points. Both teams truly knew their stuff. We were both so engaged in the match that when the all too familiar parrot voice "Time is up, time is up!" echoed, bouncing off the thin walls of the classroom and the hairs of our ears, encouraging some of us to laugh uncontrollably, we were surprised at how fast time had flown by. That was true until the points were calculated.

Daisy started humming a pretty little tune as she found the sum of the tic marks for the Sassy Girls, and in retaliation, just to be heard, Tommy hummed a more boyish tune, louder and stronger as he calculated the tic marks for the Wild Boys.

Mr. Prosper stood firmly in place by the two desks for a tiebreaker round. My guess was that he had predicted there would be another tie. His prediction was correct. Neither scorekeeper needed to tell him the answer, for he could see what was on the board and in his head.

Here we were again, in the heat of the battle, in a tiebreaker round. By the way, it would be the second and the last of its kind for the year. It was also true about Mr. Prosper, or was it? Since Mr. P. was so good at being a game show host, *would* he be invited to host the much anticipated rematch in April?

So, you want to know who won the match, and overall, who earned the bragging rights until the following April, don't you? Was it the Wild

Boys or the Sassy Girls? Apple represented the Sassy Girls and Eddie was nominated to lead the Wild Boys. This was another toe-to-toe battle. Sadly, at least to my team and me, the Sassy Girls won the match, and the overall game. They had the bragging rights, at least until next April.

Pack up, Reflection

I had a wonderful time during the Fall Festival, but somewhere in the back of my mind, I still wondered what Steve wrote during the Math Match, the match we should have won hands down if Steve had done his part as a team member by paying more attention to the equation. I remember his gloomy reaction to his incorrect answer and saw a little remorse from his lack of attention.

Yes, I know the old quote, "There is no 'I' in team, but there is in the word win." So, when your team has a player well-rehearsed, and in this case extremely great, at math, that player, (Steve), should give his utmost attention. I believe if Steve had paid more attention, we would have demolished the girls, but I also know that the saying Mrs. Fair told us, "Things happen for a reason" is also quite true.

I agree with Mr. Prosper's saying, "Everyone is a winner!" But, we children, students of Workaholic Elementary School, have always had a competitive edge and having bragging rights for even just a brief time is exciting. We never took winning out of proportion. Even the team not victorious in the five-subject matches was considered champions in their own right due to their extreme enthusiasm, competitive spirit, sportsmanship, and willingness to take a disappointing loss as a learning lesson. It gave them more of a reason to be fluent in his/her studies and to be victorious in the upcoming spring challenge.

In a fun and nagging way, a little competitive talk went back and forth that day. I heard Daisy yell, "*Good* game boys!" in a slightly sarcastic tone.

A quick retaliation from the Wild Boys was unanimously made when we hollered back in an even more sarcastic tone, "Yeah. Ha! Ha! *Thanks* Sassy Girls! We'll see *you* next April!"

Any student I know would think that Mr. Prosper would chime in and say something like "Come on now boys and girls, play nice," but that was not the case. He just sat in Mrs. Fair's comfortable chair by her desk

watching and smiling as we Wild Boys and those Sassy Girls had a little innocent teasing fun.

While all of the *nice* sarcasm was going back and forth, I decided to
write a poem about what happened that day. I left it on my desk hoping
that Mr. Prosper would see it. I hoped he would like it.

"Fall Festival"

The hallways were filled with charters
Real to imagination true
All teachers and students played their roles
To get away from math, boohoo

We paraded around the hallways
To prove that fifth grade was the best
While our heads were high in the clouds
The rest of the school was at rest

The fun we had could not be measured
By ruler, meter stick, or cup
Our jubilant sound could be heard
Up the road by a barking pup

Time came for the parade to end
But the best part was yet to come
Buffets of our favorite foods
Made our eyes scream "Yum-yum!"

Tummies were filled and minds at ease
Postpone the competition please
The next thing we knew, the game was tied
A trick by our team's enemy

The Sassy Girls were victorious
The Wild Boys' plan awry

> Grateful they were as the champions
> We Wild Boys went home with heads high

Before we dismissed for the day, we turned toward Mr. Prosper and yelled at the top of our lungs, "THANK YOU, MR. PROSPER! You are the greatest substitute ever!" We barely noticed the final cell in the column filled in on the table. I should not even have to show the table. Why? Come on, give me a break. Mr. Proper was, and still is, the best substitute teacher. Steve started and never stopped improving himself. Oh, and don't let me forget, Workaholic Elementary School is and forever will be, the best school, with an unbeatable record. On the other hand, just look at this table and see for yourself what I am bragging about.

Day 1	Food Fight
Day 2	Start of New Streak (Day 1) YES
Day 3	Continuing Streak (Day 2) YES
Day 4	Continuing Streak (Day 3) YES
Day 5	Continuing Streak (Day 4) YES
Day 6	Continuing Streak (Day 5) YES
Day 7	Continuing Streak (Day 6) YES
Day 8	Continuing Streak (Day 7) YES
Day 9	Continuing Streak (Day 8) YES
Day 10	Continuing Streak (Day 9) YES

Steve waited until everyone in the class left. I saw him get up from his seat and place two sealed envelopes on Mrs. Fair's desk. He turned around to face Mr. Prosper, waved goodbye and exited the classroom, closing the door behind him. Since my mother is a teacher here, I was the last one out of the room. I believe I saw Mr. Prosper tear up, but then I thought to myself, Triple P. would *NEVER* cry. A final thought crossed my mind, *sometimes even tough men cry.* Hailey was with me, but she did not see anything, so please keep this between you and me! Here is the letter that Steve furiously copied so he could have it to remember. He showed me one day after Mr. Prosper's assignment for Mrs. Fair was over.

Dear Mr. Prosper,

First of all, I would like to thank you for being my class's substitute teacher during the absence of Mrs. Fair. I know I did not make a very good first impression with you, but I have learned a lot since you have been here.

At my old school, neither regular teacher nor substitute teacher can compare to you. The rumors about mischievous students running ramped in the hallways and classrooms are quite true. It is not a good excuse for my behavior, but that was the atmosphere I grew up in since Kindergarten.

Thankfully my mother cared enough about me that she entered and won the school lottery. My first day with Mrs. Fair was horrible, but in retrospect, when I think about it, I was getting Highland Elementary School out of my system.

The next day, your first day on assignment, the Highland Elementary bug bit me again, resulting in the one and only Workaholic Elementary Food Fight. I do not remember anything between picking up my plate of food and arriving at Principal Paige's office. It was almost like I was under someone's control, throwing, ducking, and dodging food, and cleaning up the mess.

These past 10 days with you in my class have been an eye-opening experience for me. My old nickname, The Bee, is no longer part of me. It has nothing to do with who I am now and who I want to be. From now on, you can call me "Mr. Sting" or "Steve-O" and everybody else can call me the latter of the two. The "O" is for: *oh my, look how that young man has changed*, and *oh my, I wish my boy could grow up to be like him*!

Thank you for such a wonderful Fall Festival. For a second there, I thought I felt a little Highland bug bite me, but the reflection I saw, or thought I saw of Triple P. was just enough of the cure I needed. Thank you for the positive influence you had on me. I thought to myself, which is more enjoyable: *being part of the fun* or *making a spectacle of myself, therefore ruining the fun of hundreds*!

A second thought popped into my head, *really, Steve, how much fun do you actually have making those around you miserable?*

One final thought hit me before the Fall Festival ended. It became clear to me during lunch that you and Triple P. are one and the same. I put the pieces together when you left class and Triple P. would show up. Please don't worry; your secret is safe with me. I think Gregory knows, but no need to worry because he won't say anything either.

You and Triple P. have been such a positive influence on me. I have no idea how to repay you for what you have done. All I can really say is, THANK YOU VERY MUCH FROM THE BOTTOM OF MY HEART!

PS: I hope to see you at Workaholic Middle School!

Sincerely,
Steve-O Sting

Chapter 18

Mrs. Fair Returns

ONE OF THE first things Mrs. Fair saw when she returned that Monday was a sealed envelope stuffed with a personalized letter from Steve. I would never share a letter like this unless I had permission from the writer, and for this I do. Please read this endearing letter.

Dear Mrs. Fair,

Allow me to be the first student to welcome you back from your 10 day visit with your sister and new nephew.

I sincerely apologize for my inappropriate behavior on my first day of school here. I remember from your reaction that it was totally disrespectful. The reason, albeit horrible, was to help keep up my now, **former** reputation.

Principal Paige let me know how my behavior would not be tolerated here at Workaholic Elementary School. A day at home where I could do anything I wanted was exactly my plan at the time. I thought to myself, *a day off from school and the house to myself!* Little did I know, my mother and I did not view the situation the same. She got an earful from Principal Paige when she picked me up that day. Luckily, not to embarrass me too much at school, she let me know how she personally felt when we got in her car. My punishment was *house arrest in my room.* This house detention felt worse than detention at school. The only time I could leave was to go to the bathroom or to get something to eat.

These past 10 days have been an eye opener for me. Mr. Prosper taught me a lot. You probably already knew that from his daily notes sent to you. From this point forward, I will no longer be a problem student for you or any substitute teacher.

One major thing I learned was that all the attention I sought and received was negative attention. I was so used to acting up like that with little consequence at my old school that I thought about trying it here.

From now on, please call me Steve-O. If that won't work, plain old Steve or Mr. Sting will work. I will no longer be known as The Bee because that name brings negativity. The "O" at the end of my name means, *oh, think of the possibilities with that young man!* My enclosed acrostic poem will explain more of who I am now. My oath to you:

For the rest of my time here at Workaholic Elementary School, I, Steve-O Sting, will cause neither you, nor anyone else here, heartache, nor be a pain in the buttocks, nor any other body part. If, for some unforeseen reason, I break my oath, I, Steve-O Sting, shall serve the number of hours of detention that match the day of the school record. If that consequence shall not suffice, I will accept any given alternative. I will do anything to keep the school record going.

Sincerely,
Steve-O Sting

Enclosures: Poems

PS: If there is a day that you will be absent, please do whatever it takes to get Mr. Prosper to fill in for you. Thank you ahead of time!

"UNIQUENESS"

We are unique in our own way
Just as the sky changes today

Tall, thin, short, fat, hairy or bald
Pimples or clear, brace face, head gear

Glasses or not, much better to see
Please, oh please, do not judge me

I am like you, and you are like me
In many ways, we are the same

For the most part, we are unique
I accept you, and you accept me

One day real soon, we'll celebrate
Uniqueness, it does define us all

"Steve-O"

Staying focused
Through the school day
Evaluating every circumstance
Valuing everything given to me
Encouraging others around me to always be positive
-
Oh, the endless possibilities I have

One day during writing, we worked on acrostic poems. Steve made a copy of his poem and placed it in the envelope with his letter to Mrs. Fair.

Chapter 19
Post Mr. Prosper's Assignment

BEFORE I GO on about the rest of the school year, I want to tell you about what my friends and I did for Halloween. A few friends and I had a sleepover at my house. We stayed up late talking, watching horror movies, and eating candy. We did not eat as much as we wanted to because my mother took our bags after about two hours. None of us could move one inch after the amount of candy we ate.

After sleeping for ten hours, my mother finally woke us up for breakfast. Even though the French toast, fried eggs, and orange juice looked mouthwatering, neither my friends nor I were very hungry. We barely ate our bowls of apple cinnamon oatmeal my mother had cooked especially for us. We even turned down my mother's famous Halloween chocolate stuffed pastries.

When it was time for my friends to go home, my mother smiled while handing each of them their bag of candy saying, "Here is your bag. I hope you feel better soon. It would be a shame to waste such a beautiful day. Call Gregory when you're ready to play."

November and December came and went by in the blink of an eye. Since this story is about Mr. Prosper, I will not bore you with any of the non-important details. No fifth grader saw Mr. P. in the hallways during that time. We heard a few stories about him paying a visit to some of the lower grades, but it could not be confirmed. Oh, the school streak was never broken, ending the calendar year on Day 39, the last day before our two-week Christmas Break. You have to remember, we had one week off for Thanksgiving and two weeks off for Christmas. If you haven't had them already, I hope they were/are wonderful.

Now, you do remember this tale is about Mr. Prosper, the best substitute teacher ever, and how he made a difference in many of our lives, don't you? You may not realize it, but teachers, even substitute teachers, notice a lot more than we students realize. The things they realize help them mold us into the people we will later become. That can happen ONLY if we listen to them.

As I stated earlier, Mr. Prosper had other assignments at this school, but what happened there is another story. I do not have time to go into full details right now, but I will tell you of some instances where the Punisher showed up, why he did, and the end result.

I had you going there for a minute, didn't I? Mr. Prosper actually did a lot of substituting after his ten-day assignment with us ended and from January to May, also. If you think he did a lot for my class, just you wait until you hear what he did for the whole school.

Thanksgiving

The next holiday on the list was Thanksgiving. The Friday before the belly-filling break started, there was a banquet of sorts for the teachers and staff. It was nothing big; at least that was what my mother told me. I heard rumors that Mr. Prosper cooked the turkey and a few other sides. I think he even made a couple of deserts: fudge and moist chocolate chunk cookies. Other teachers brought sides, too.

While the teachers partook in the cornucopia of food, Mr. Prosper was kind enough to stand in for them. Each grade level did its own Thanksgiving project. Some parents volunteered to make the day go easier. Mr. Prosper arrived in each grade dressed as a pilgrim carrying a book on the history of Thanksgiving. Any question asked, he knew the answer to. He even knew some answers that our regular teachers did not know.

When he came to the fifth grade hallway, we were all happy to see him. He had not been on our hall since his assignment for Mrs. Fair. Daisy was walking back to the room from getting a drink of water when she saw him turning the corner from the main hallway to ours. She kicked it into high gear running back to class hollering at the top of her lungs, "Mr. Prosper is coming! Mr. Prosper is coming!" as she entered the room.

"No, he's not! Stop kidding around!" Tommy hollered back.

With her hands on her hips, Daisy replied, "If you don't believe me, take a look for *yourself!*" in a sassy way.

Before anyone could move an inch, the classroom door opened, and lo and behold, Mr. Prosper walked into the room all decked out in his pilgrim getup. He looked like an exact replica from our history and story books.

It was around eleven AM when he arrived. He greeted us with "Good morning class. I am happy to see you again!" and then walked over to my teacher and said, "Mrs. Fair, I am here to stand in for you while you get some food from the library. Hope you enjoy. Oh, and can you bring me a couple of cookies, please?"

Mrs. Fair slowly got up from her cushiony chair, waved goodbye to us, and announced, "Class, see you in just a bit. Mr. Prosper, thank you for standing in for me, and yes, I will bring you a couple of cookies."

Questions galore were shouted throughout the class. "One at a time, please," Mr. Prosper requested. He quickly added, "I'll answer any question about Thanksgiving. All other questions will have to wait for another time."

We quickly answered with a slightly dismal, "Okay."

As I said before, any question about Thanksgiving he promptly answered. He even knew a few answers that Mrs. Fair did not know, and that was a first for me because I thought she knew everything about anything.

He left as soon as Mrs. Fair returned. On his way out the door, Mr. P. waved and called out, "Gobble, gobble! I will see you soon, fifth graders."

December

The week before Christmas break, teachers had an anonymous gift exchange thing going on. Each participating teacher drew a name from a hat. The first four days were small gifts with a spending limit of five dollars. On the fifth day, teachers would get together after school and have their big gift exchange. There was a spending limit of twenty dollars. Mr. Prosper was the delivery man, dressed in full elf attire. He could have easily been mistaken for one of Santa's elves. No need to worry, he was not left out in the receiving of gifts. I would say he was not only on Santa's good list, but also

Principal Paige's. For fulfilling his duties as a substitute teacher beyond the call of duty, Mr. Prosper received the best gift of all, a box full of cards expressing love and gratitude. The numerous bags of chocolate were the cherry on top. It took him three trips back and forth from the main office to his red 4 X 4 truck with black trim and huge tires to load everything. He had a truck side step bar installed so he could get into the front seat.

School was not the only place I saw him in his elf costume. During Christmas break, my mother and I made several trips to the mall to go shopping. Yes, I went shopping with my mom. As we rounded the corner after filling up with slices of pizza and brownies, I saw Santa and his elves. At first glance, I thought I saw someone I recognized. Upon second glance, I recognized one of the elves. It was none other than Mr. Prosper. Mom took me to see Santa so I could tell him what I wanted for Christmas.

After I sat in Santa's lap and told him what I wanted, his first elf, Mr. Prosper, leaned in and whispered, "Merry Christmas, Mr. Gaines. See you next year."

If you were worried about Steve, please don't be. The entire fifth grade class had only good things to say about him. Everyone believed Steve had become a new person and seeing was believing. I knew I was not the only one who thought something magnificent must have happened during Mr. Prosper's 10-day assignment. Whatever it was, we were happy for it!

Like I told you before, one day during music class, we found out that Steve could really belt out some outrageous notes. He was at the same level as Gail. Mr. Prosper could probably take a few notes from them. After that day, when Mr. Chord and Mr. P. called Steve's mother and told her they knew Steve was a great singer, Steve became one of the lead vocals of the Workaholic Elementary School Fifth Grade Ensemble, which performed at the Second Annual WES Holiday Recital. Only Steve and a few other students had solo parts.

During the recital, there was a special guest. Guess who it was. Correct! It was none other than Mr. Prosper himself. Do you remember him belting out a few things while hosting the series of matches in Mrs. Fair's class? Well, he did even better that night. He received a standing ovation, which lasted three minutes. Do you know a substitute who has the vocal chords of Mr. Prosper and has been invited to perform at a recital?

His opening act was a difficult one to follow, but my classmates and I were up for the challenge. Don't get me wrong, he was the best substitute teacher ever, but there was a reason this was called the WES Fifth Grade Ensemble. It was about us, the fifth graders. Well, we stepped up to the plate and hit a grand slam. Steve, Gail, Hailey, and Pete, yes Pete, added their performance as a quartet, the first one of any of the past fifth grade classes. Our standing ovation lasted an astounding seven minutes. It was the longest of any performance that day, even Mr. Prosper's.

February

I skipped January because nothing worth talking about happened. Other than celebrating New Year's Day by staying up late banging pots and pans at twelve AM, the day flew by quickly. It was one of the few nights I was permitted to stay up past my bedtime. Most girls I know love the month of February because of the special day, Saint Valentine's Day. Mr. Prosper did something I never thought he would do. The week of this special holiday, he dressed up as Cupid while delivering special packages to the teachers.

March

This month went by quickly, too, just like January. I did not hear too much about Mr. Prosper. Perhaps the other schools had heard about him and wanted him to come work some of his magic. The only thing I remember about this month was *Spring break*. Since my mother and I had this week off, she made sure my father had it off from his job, too. We did a *family thing* that I will keep to myself.

April

I'm going to keep this month short. The Sassy Girls won the first set of matches against the Wild Boys back in October, but only by a slim margin. On the last Friday in April, the rematch took place. Mrs. Fair could have been the host, but even she knew that we needed Mr. Prosper. A week prior to *Game Day*, Mrs. Fair made arrangements with Mr. Prosper to come and be the host. Of course, he graciously accepted the offer.

Since it was April, the weather a little warmer, his suit was lighter in color. That day he wore a powder blue jacket and pants to match, a light yellow long sleeve dress shirt, a solid pink tie to match, and his trusty black shoes and dress socks. You better believe he brought his karaoke machine and microphone, too.

This showdown did not take place in class. No, it took place in the hallway where all the other fifth graders could be spectators and see Mr. Prosper's magic. Mr. Prosper dug even deeper into his so-called *bag of tricks*. His stage presence in front of the crowd was even more impressive than it was back in October when he put on a show for us in Mrs. Fair's class. To make this long story short, the Wild Boys demolished the Sassy Girls by winning all five matches. No tiebreaker rounds were needed. Some of you girls may have thought the Sassy Girls took it easy on us Wild Boys, but you would have been highly mistaken.

For a moment, we did our happy dance and chanted, "Wild Boys! Wild Boys! Wild Boys!" as we danced around the hallway. I guess that was our way of rubbing it into their wounds. After about two minutes we stopped and shook hands with the Sassy Girls. This set of matches proved that boys are just as smart as girls, possibly even smarter. We all have strong and weak places, but when we work together, the boundaries are limitless.

But anyway, Mr. Prosper put on a spectacular show, and Mrs. Fair, along with the other fifth grade teachers, could not stop talking about him after school that day. I heard he had been booked solid for the rest of that school year and the next three. Teachers will do anything in a positive way to get students to learn, especially when it involves the best substitute teacher ever, Mr. Prosper.

May

Two very important things happened that month—the fifth grade field trip to Coaster Haven on the first Friday and the school-wide field day on the second Friday. You probably already guessed it by now; Mr. Prosper played an important role in each event.

Fifth Grade Field Trip

There we were, every single fifth grader, standing in the bus arrival and departure area with his/her teacher. A few parents, and yes, Mr. Prosper, too, stood with us as chaperones for the field trip. This trip was the main thing on our minds for the past few days.

We went to Coaster Haven where the most extreme roller coasters for the adventurous to the smaller coasters for the beginners exist. Old carnival games such as popping balloons with darts, throwing a ball to knock down bowling pins, water games, and a wonderful arcade full of video games of years past that Mom and Dad played, set the atmosphere.

You heard what I said, "Every fifth grade student, even Steve, went on this fantastic field trip filled to the brim with indescribable feelings."

The only reason I could think of why Mr. Prosper went with us was because we all begged and pleaded with our teachers and Principal Paige to invite him. I don't know if they gave in, or if they planned on inviting him anyway. The exact reason doesn't really matter. All that mattered to the fifth grade was that the best substitute teacher ever, Mr. Prosper, was with us.

Some people may have thought that Steve saw this as an opportunity to revert back to his old antics, but the thought never crossed his mind. Steve had turned over a new leaf, actually too many to count. He was possibly even growing a new tree with respect to the new boy he had morphed into. The bus was no place for any person to be imprisoned for bad behavior, not even the bus driver.

Upon arrival, we trickled out of the buses in an orderly flow. Each chaperon guided a set number of students throughout the park. I was grouped with Steve, Hailey, Pete, Zac, Alice, and Francis. Luckily, Mr. Prosper was our chaperon. I had a gut feeling we were going to have fun.

I saw a side of Mr. Prosper I had never seen at school, an extremely fun side. No matter how scary the ride, he rode with us. Mr. P. played all the carnival games we played, and he even showed us how to play some old video games he had played when he was younger. There was a claw machine in the corner of the arcade, and nobody who played it could ever win a prize. This was not the case for Mr. Prosper. Every single time he deposited his fifty cents into the machine he would win. Mr. P. came out of the arcade with at least twelve stuffed and furry prizes.

Afterward, we approached a game with a billiard table. The past few summers, when I had visited my uncle, he would take me to the billiard hall for a couple of hours before going for hamburgers or a movie. He taught me how to play this game he called *pool*. My uncle showed me everything about the game. He showed me the cue ball, cue stick, balls (solids and stripes), names of pockets, and told me that the term *break* was the moment the cue ball made contact with all of the other balls formed in a triangle at one end of the table while the cue ball was hit with the cue stick from the other end. I had picked up the game like I was a mini pro. They called me "Sneaky G." because nobody would ever suspect someone my size or age could be so good at the game.

In the game at the park, a cue ball sat at one end of the table and three balls connected in the shape of a triangle sat at the other end. After paying the game attendant my two dollars, I was handed a pool stick. I lathered the tip with some blue chalk, bent down over the table, dotted the cue ball with an invisible dot, pulled the stick back, and hit the dot with it. The balls scattered in all directions. Before making my first of three shots, I looked at all possible shots on the table. Using everything my uncle had taught me, I approached the table with cue stick in hand to make my first shot. I pulled the cue stick back, made contact with the cue ball, and it rolled down the table and hit one of the other balls resulting in it falling into a pocket. I went through the same motions the next two times, successfully sinking the last two balls in different pockets. The winning felt so good that I did it again and won two stuffed animals.

On our way to the food court we came across one of those basketball games where the player shoots the basketball from a marked line into the basketball hoop. I already knew that Francis had some mean basketball skills, so he walked ahead of us to prove it. Sadly, he failed each of his two attempts.

Mr. Prosper watched in dismay with the rest of us. Something must have popped into his mind when he approached Francis and gave some advice. Mr. Prosper gave the game attendant his two dollars, set his feet firmly behind the line, gave the basketball a couple bounces, slowly lifted the ball to his eyes to aim, and then let the ball go. It flew through the air with a perfect arc; when it landed dead solid in the hoop, it made a *swish* sound.

"Nice shot, sir!" yelled the game attendant, congratulating Mr. Prosper for making such a beautiful shot. The next thing heard: "What color basketball would you like?"

Mr. P. looked at us and asked, "What color would you guys like?"

Francis looked at the rest of us, and unanimously we happily yelled, "The red one!"

As soon as Mr. P. rejoined us, I asked, "If I give you two dollars, would you shoot the ball for me?"

Being the nice guy that he is, Mr. Prosper graciously accepted, walked up to the same game attendant, handed her the money, went through the same motions, and made another flawless shot. Mr. Prosper was on a hot streak. I would not have written this if it wasn't so impressive. Mr. P. continued his streak by doing the same for Steve, Hailey, Pete, Zac, and Alice. Each of us had our own basketball!

Three spectators asked Mr. Prosper to shoot for them. Since Mr. P. has never turned down a polite offer, he accepted their request. The last shot made was the tenth one in a row without missing. After that last amazing shot, a lead park attendant, who had been watching the entire time from just a short distance away, approached us. He said, "Excuse me, sir, how are you doing today? My name is Carl, and what I just witnessed there was amazing, and is also a park record."

We all stood frozen in amazement while Mr. Prosper just smiled. He replied, "Well, nice to meet you, Carl. My name is Mr. Prosper, but my students call me Mr. P."

They shook hands as Carl asked, "Will you please walk with me so we can get a picture of you to place on our wall? You see, there is a camera on each basketball game, and pictures are taken for players to have an opportunity to purchase."

Mr. Prosper followed Carl to a covered area full of pictures of previous record holders. We trailed behind him like zombies.

Carl walked behind the counter, pulled two pictures out of the printer, looked at Mr. P. and asked, "If you will please, Mr. Prosper, may I have your autograph across this picture."

All of us watched this memorable moment as Mr. Prosper autographed the picture and watched Carl place it into a picture frame, then loop the string on the highest nail on the Wall of Fame. Of course, Mr. Prosper signed the second picture, which was also placed in a picture frame. A decorative plate was attached to the bottom with the inscription,

COASTER HAVEN BASKETBALL RECORD HOLDER. 10 SHOTS MADE IN A ROW.

Now we had a reason to be hungry. All of us pitched in to buy one pizza with everything on it, several 24-ounce water bottles because it was so hot that day, and ice cream in a bowl so it wouldn't melt all over us. After that rather large meal, we walked around the park looking for some of our classmates. The group we found looked tired too, so we all got on one last *easy ride.* We had already had enough excitement for the day. It was getting late and time for all fifth graders and chaperons to meet at the front of the park to get on the buses. After each class did its head count, the buses were loaded, and the trip back to school began. Try to imagine if you can the conversations we had on the bus ride home!

You probably had a fifth grade field trip at your school. Whatever you do, do not forget what you did. If you will, write it down in a journal. Yes, boys do have journals. Girls just call theirs a diary. So, it is not *girly* for a boy to write down his memories. It just may be handy some day when he wants to review what he did some time ago.

School-Wide Field Day

It was that time of the school year, the time every child loves. It was the second Friday in May, the last day to really have fun and blow off some steam. We called this event the School-Wide Field Day. See if you find any similarities between my field day and yours. You never know, there may just be something you would like to have at your field day. Just so you don't forget, write down how much fun you had, and if possible take some pictures. Not to spoil any of the fun, but we all know that the next week would be testing.

This is a time to put your thinking cap on and dig deep into your imagination to see what my school did for field day. There were both indoor and outdoor activities. Every single student, yes, even Steve-O, partook in the festivities. We had nothing but fun.

For those students who liked the indoors more than the outdoors, a few teachers and parent volunteers were ready to make their day indoors as much fun as his/her classmates spending most of the day outside. A couple of rooms had various songs playing for dance, one room had a cupcake walk, and another room played musical chairs. I even heard of a few students playing hide and go seek. One of the parent volunteers who loved art was given permission by the art teacher, Mrs. Mastery, to use some of the paint for finger painting, and some of the colored pencils for drawing.

Those who loved being outside on days like this, me included, had a blast. We did not even think about the few nameless classmates that stayed inside. Think about it for a minute.

The bright golden sun lighting up the cloudless blue sky, giving off just enough heat, the sound of children of all ages yelling, running, and playing all morning, and pausing just for a moment to eat lunch. There was no other day that could compare to this.

My class started the day off playing three games of Four Square at the same time, not even keeping track of who won and who lost. After our time there, it was off to play parachute. It had balls of various sizes and colors; you know the game. Next, we had an extended time in the main area where we played kickball, softball toss, airplane toss, and disc golf. We also bought snacks with tickets. While most of us stayed in this area a little longer, a few of the runners went up to the flat grassy area for a 50-yard dash and a 75-yard dash. I didn't know, nor did I care, who won the races. We were outside to have some fun.

Before we knew it, lunch time had arrived. Bagged lunches were waiting on the tables in the cafeteria with teacher names on them. Quickly we grabbed them and headed back to our class to eat and watch part of a movie. Waiting in the class was Mr. Prosper. I got so caught up in having fun I forgot to keep an eye on him.

The first thing out of his mouth was, "Hello boys and girls. I am very happy to see you guys again!"

All at once we replied, "Hi, Mr. Prosper, how are you doing?" in soft, tired voices.

He looked at us in confusion knowing that we are usually more energetic than that. Next, in an exhilarating voice, "Come on now! I know you boys and girls have more energy than that!" sending a jolt of energy up and down our spines.

Our second greeting, "HELLO, MR. PROSPER!" was louder than before.

The next thing I knew, he pulled out something from his bag of tricks. It just happened to be individual-sized almond butter chunk chocolate ice cream. This treat not only tasted out of this world, it was also packed with protein and calcium, just the stuff we needed to face our next class challenges, which were three legged races, tug-of-war, and water balloon fights.

By the time it came for us to partake in our first challenge, the three-legged races, we were still a little full from that wonderful treat Mr. Prosper had given us. Sadly, we moved at a snail's pace and lost, but we had a blast, and that was all that mattered.

All that laughter and extra walking did the trick to help digest that special treat. Our next challenge, one of the most important ones, was the class tug-of-war. Two classes were called up to face one another. The victors would proceed onto the next challenge. Teachers played in the anchor position at the end of the rope. We begged and pleaded with Mrs. Fair to allow Mr. P. to take her place. She wiped the brow of her head and gladly accepted the offer. Mr. Prosper was excited to be on our team.

Our first opponent was Mr. Augment's class. They put up a valiant fight, but we came out victorious. For a moment there, they had us begging, "Don't pull so hard! We give …"

Suddenly I, who was in the middle of the pack, felt the rope being pulled more towards our end. I heard Mr. Prosper shout several times "PULL! One, two, three, PULL!" On the word, *pull,* we all pulled as hard as we could. In less than a minute, the red ribbon in the middle of the rope had passed the line, declaring us victorious.

On our way to the sideline to rest and watch the next two classes go at it, I could have sworn that I saw some veins bursting out of Mr. Prosper's arms. Who knew that someone his size had muscles as strong as he did? Perhaps, he was just putting on a show for us all this past year, pretending he was not very strong. This goes to show you, *never judge a book by its cover,* and *always be cautious of the quiet student!* My class, with Mr. Prosper as the anchor, went on to win the rest of our matches. No trophy was given. In its place, we received five extra water balloons for each team member.

These extra water balloons were needed for the end of the day schoolwide water balloon fight. Please don't worry, this was explained in the permission note. Everyone had extra clothing to change into after the fun and exciting water balloon fights. There was no ultimate winner. A few of us got back at Steve for the food fight earlier in the year. He expected this and was well prepared himself because locating him was like finding a needle in a massive haystack. The few times he dared to show his face, Pete was nearby ready to attack. Even though Steve and I had become friends over the year, I could not help myself. I just had to give Pete my extra water balloons before I went inside to change. Steve never knew I had done that, so please don't tell him.

Sadly, the fun ended with whistles blowing all over the playground, ending the first ever school-wide water balloon fight. On second thought, I made a guess that it was only allowed by administration because of our new, and still going, streak where no student had been sent to Principal Paige's office. Every student quickly made their way inside to change to go home. It probably was one of the smoothest transitions to end school I had ever been a part of.

Chapter 20

The End! No, Not Really

FINALLY, IT WAS the last day of school before summer break and vivid visions of playing baseball, soccer, football, cheerleading camp, basketball, going to the neighborhood pool, family reunions, and of course family vacations to the beach filled the students' minds across all grade levels throughout the school day.

A *buzz-buzz, crackle-crackle* ear-piercing sound from the loudspeaker bombarded us as we all covered our ears. Our wonderful Principal Paige closed out the day by giving her yearly *End of the School Year* speech (too boring for me to tell you about) and then turned over the intercom system to the school's amateur radio host.

The next thing we heard was "This is Hailey Halen sounding off for station WMALR. Students and teachers of Workaholic Elementary School, it has been my pleasure to bring you magnificent songs. Please enjoy this last set of songs as I rejoin my fellow fifth graders" and she played *I Got the Homework Itch.*

Hailey packed things up for the summer while the song was playing and heard the *ring-ring, ring-ring* of the station phone. It startled her so much that she just about fell back into her comfortable and cushiony chair with her initials inscribed on the back, *H.H. Radio.* She listened to the anonymous caller intensely and could not believe the shocking news. She quickly replied, "Hold on now, wait a minute there, mister," placed the caller on hold, and frantically interrupted the song.

Boys and girls of Workaholic Elementary School, do I have a fantastic surprise for you. I just received fantastic news directly through the Highlyprankablevine that Mr. Prosper will indeed be a substitute teacher next year at Workaholic Middle School. That is fantastic news for all fifth graders. We all have heard the horror stories about how difficult sixth grade can be. We will be in class with many other fifth grade students from the *other* elementary schools.

Before returning to her conversation with the anonymous caller, she announced, "Now, back to your regularly scheduled song!"

Going with her gut instinct, Hailey questioned, "Wait a minute. Who is this? Are you sure?" She could not quite recognize the voice because it was muffled from one of those things found in a joke store.

In reply to Hailey's question, the voice said in a dastardly way, "*Guess?*"

The first thing that came to her mind was Steve. Then Hailey answered, "*Oh no*, it is you, Steve!"

Gleaming from ear to ear, Steve instantly answered, "You are absolutely, one hundred percent correct!" Without hesitation, Steve whispered into the phone, "Hailey, guess what?"

Slipping farther and farther down her chair, Hailey dramatically begged, "*Please* don't say it! I beg you, Steve, *please* don't say it!"

Disregarding her plea, Steve replied, "You just got Stung!" followed by "Sting you here, sting you there. Watch your back, because you never know where!"

This was something neither she nor anybody else had ever heard Steve say before, and that was scary.

Immediately, Hailey screamed into the phone, "*Really*, Steve! I thought you had *changed!*"

Quickly, before Hailey could say anything else, Steve cackled, "Just kidding, Hailey. I just *had* to get it out of my system for good. I sincerely apologize."

Hailey let out a scream that could awaken the dearly departed. Luckily, her microphone was *not* on at the time. Sorrowfully, Hailey interrupted the next song, *Guess the Answer* with:

Please pardon this interruption. Students at Workaholic
Elementary School, the caller who told me that Mr. Prosper
would be a substitute teacher at Workaholic Middle School was a
prank by none other than Steve Sting. I am extremely sorry for
the inconvenience.

We are the Beavers started to play as Hailey closed the door to the radio
station in the audio/video room. Her footsteps were in perfect sync to the
beats of the song. Finally, Hailey arrived at Mrs. Fair's class. Without hesitation, she joined her friends in all the fun and festivities of taking pictures,
singing to her groovy tunes, signing yearbooks, saying goodbyes to teachers,
and telling each other of summer plans.

So, how did Steve get ahold of a school phone you ask? Well, since it
was the last day of school, students were permitted to walk around their
hallway to talk to other students and get his or her yearbook signed. There
just happened to be a vacant room used for various projects during the
year, and the door was unlocked. Being the sly guy Steve could sometimes
be, he made sure the coast was clear and had made his call. I guess he got
so into his prank call that he forgot to watch his back.

Just as Steve hung up the telephone and turned around to exit the
room, he saw standing behind him the one and only Triple P. Steve started
to panic and stutter, "I, I, wa, was, ju, just, pl, pla, playing around." Steve
Sting had never stuttered before.

The Pick-on People Punisher just smiled because he saw and heard
everything Steve had said. Triple. P. motioned to Steve for him to come
closer, and he whispered something in his ear.

Immediately, Steve snapped out of it, clearing his voice while his
clever little smile returned. He looked directly into the eyes of Triple P. and
whispered, "Why, hello there, Mr. Prosper."

In his deep, raspy voice Mr. P. replied, "Mr. Sting, you are dearly mistaken. It is I, Triple P., Pick-on People Punisher, also known as P. to the
Third Power. I do not know where Mr. Prosper is."

With that all too familiar smirk still frozen to his face, Steve rebutted,
"Come on, Mr. Prosper! I know it is you!"

The Punisher leaned close to Steve's ear and ever so silently said, "How are you doing, Steve? Now you know that you are wrong for teasing Hailey like that, don't you?" as he handed Steve a consequence letter.

"Yes sir, I do know," Steve kindly replied.

Triple P. added, "You owe her a sincere apology!"

"Yes, sir, you are absolutely correct," Steve said, nodding his head up and down.

Since it was the last day of school, Triple P., or was it Mr. Prosper, must have been in a good mood because the so called *Consequence Letter* was BLANK. How do I know this? Well, Steve showed it to me. Steve and I agreed that it was given to let him know how it felt to be teased. Plus, even teachers have to have fun every now and then. Yes, I called Mr. Prosper, who we knew as the best substitute teacher ever, a teacher! Anyone who can get Steve, now Steve-O, to change is by all means considered a teacher to me!

Steve waved at Triple P. as he exited the dark, vacant room leaving him behind hiding from everyone. He probably was changing quickly back into Mr. Prosper, so he could wave goodbye to the entire fifth grade class and the rest of the students. As Steve walked toward all the fun noise to say his goodbyes to his classmates, he passed by Hailey. Without hesitation, she gave him a stern look and socked him dead center on his arm for the prank call. Steve rubbed his arm and smiled as they each went in separate directions.

Mr. P. decided to stop by the radio station as he made his final rounds on the last day of the school year. Right before the last song on the play list, *See You Next Year*, began, a "Testing, one, two, is this thing on?" startled us all as we gathered our personal belongings. Mr. Prosper sat comfortably in Hailey's chair and closed out the school year with:

To all you fabulous fifth graders, I hope you have a wonderful summer! Good luck in middle school. If you want to know if I previously substituted or will be a substitute teacher at Workaholic Middle School, just ask your older brother or sister. *Maybe* I will see you there, and *maybe* I won't!

That final sign-off by Mr. Prosper blew our minds. We pondered the question even more: *Will Mr. Prosper be a substitute teacher at Workaholic Middle School?* For some of us, that question resulted in several sleepless nights. It would especially bother us the week before middle school was to start.

The last day of school went by so fast! Before Steve or even I knew it, the final bell of the school year chimed. Yes, even I, the *quiet one*, had a lot of fun the last day of school; I came out of my shell a bit. You probably have seen in a movie when students come running out on the last day of school shouting at the top of their lungs and throwing books and things high up in the air, haven't you? Well, this is not that type of school, and for a good reason. We, even at our young age, have been taught to respect everything we have been given. Besides, we blew off a lot of steam last week at the school-wide field day. Oh, and we would also have a chance to throw our caps up in the air at the fifth grade graduation ceremony.

Steve and I had become friends throughout the year. His mother had bought a house one short block down the street from me. He and I decided to walk home, knowing that it would take longer than the bus or even waiting for my mother to take us, but we really wanted to see our friends who lived closer and wave at all the school buses that buzzed by. The thought of the possibility of seeing Mr. Prosper next year at Workaholic Middle School remained on our minds as we hiked the one mile distance up hill. Even though I only heard of him subbing in elementary schools, his last words remained on my mind. Additionally, I have never heard any older boy or girl in the neighborhood talk about him.

Walking home, I silently thought, *so, will Steve's prank become reality, or was it just a prank?* Steve stopped briefly to wave goodbye to me as he high-tailed it to his house. Both of us had to take a quick shower and then dress up for the graduation ceremony, which was to be held promptly at six PM.

Fifth grade students arrived back at school at five PM dressed sharply. Before the final show began, graduates sat in seats marked with a personalized envelope and card. Teachers were also dressed in their Sunday best. Parent volunteers from the PTO stayed behind at the end of school to finish decorating the cafeteria for the graduation and awards ceremony.

Now, I don't want to bother you with all the boring details, so I won't. Just wait until you have your ceremony, or if you already had yours, think back to how it felt to finally graduate from elementary school and make it to middle school.

Mr. Prosper was such a positive influence on us, the entire fifth grade, we decided to pitch in and create an acrostic poem for him from the bottom of our hearts. It was created while he was saying his own farewells to teachers and staff, and giving his last speech for the year over the intercom to us fifth graders. I am pretty sure he saw this poem after we went home to change into our clothes for the ceremony. If you ask any of us, we believe that his eyes quite possibly did tear up. There was no grade on it, being the last day of school, but we still gave it our all. We dug deeper into the creative parts of our brains, deeper than we had ever dug before, to create this beautiful acrostic poem about Mr. Prosper, and it goes something like this:

"Mr. Prosper"

Magnificent skills he possesses, many unknown to students
Runt in size to some, but giant in heart to care for others

.

Peaceful is how he runs the class every day
Reliable to those who need him
Observing all goings on under his care
Sensitive to everyone's feelings
Pondering he keeps our minds growing
Enduring love for our academic and social growth
Resourceful in using tools necessary for our success

We, the entire fifth grade, nominated Mr. Prosper for the *Substitute of the Year* award. He won it by an enormous landslide, no need for a second vote. The other substitute teachers pretty much knew that he would win. Of course, you know that he showed up for the ceremony and that the award was a total surprise to him. He was none the wiser that the entire fifth grade body of Workaholic Elementary School voted on such a matter.

Thanks to Mr. Prosper, being the great substitute teacher he is, we the fifth grade class were able to leave Workaholic Elementary School with a school record of 124 days of no student being sent to Principal Paige's office—a record that I am sure will never be broken!

SUBSTITUTE OF THE YEAR

THE BEST SUBSTITUTE EVER
MR. PROSPER

Well, you heard Hailey sign off the radio for the last time, so now it's my turn. Please wish my friends and me well in middle school, and I will do the same for you. I sure hope it is not as scary as what I have heard it to be.

Way down, deep in the back of my mind, I hope Mr. Prosper will be a substitute teacher at Workaholic Middle School, because if it does get bad, I know he, I mean Triple P. of course, would straighten things out.

"I do too!" Steve just yelled in my ear.

Now, nobody else here knows that Triple P. is actually Mr. Prosper. You have to make a promise to Steve and me that you will keep Mr. Prosper's secret identity top secret! Steve and I made a promise between ourselves. Now it's your turn. Do you see the two hands with pinkies out? Hold your pinky out and shake both of them. We now have a *Pinky Promise* between us; you will *not* tell anyone about Mr. Prosper.

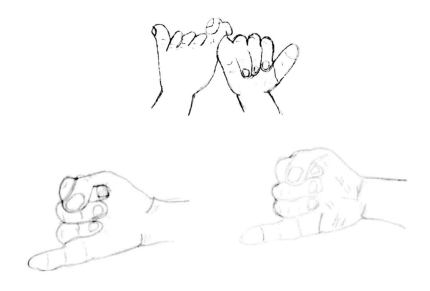

CPSIA information can be obtained
at www.ICGtesting.com
Printed in the USA
FFOW03n0051071215
19347FF

9 781942 899549